This book is a work of [...]
places and incidents ei[...]
author's imagination c[...]
resemblance to actu[...]
events or locales is entirely co[...]

Copyright © 2024 by C. M. Kent

All rights reserved. No part of this book may be reproduced or used in any manner without written permission of the copyright owner except for the use of quotations in a book review.

For more information,
Email: c.m.kent.publishing@gmail.com

First Paperback Edition April 2nd, 2024

Book design by C. M. Kent

Torn Apart

By

C. M. Kent

Also by C. M. Kent

Love Novel Series

Love & Destiny
Falling
Truly, Madly, Deeply
Heavenly
Love & Heartbreak
Bound 2 Love
Crazy in Love
Just Us
Love & Devastation
Torn Apart

Miami Connections Novel Series

Miami Connections: Secrets and Lies.
Part One
Miami Connections: Secrets and Lies.
Part Two

Miami Connections: The Domino
Effect. Part One
Miami Connections: The Domino
Effect. Part Two
Miami Connections: Redemption. Part
One
Miami Connections. Redemption. Part
Two
Miami Connections: Liberation. Part
One
Miami Connections: Liberation. Part
Two
Miami Connections: Peace, Love, &
Retribution. Part One
Miami Connections: Peace, Love, &
Retribution. Part Two

Playlists relating to all books
available on Spotify
C. M. Kent (Author)

***Even during the darkest of times,
you can still find light.***

Chapter 1
Monday, April 2nd, 2018
Miami, Florida

Sitting at his desk, what was once the center of his universe, Enrique has come to the realization that he now has nothing, nothing because he has just made the biggest mistake of his life; he's just let Kristie, his only true love, walk out of his life and he did absolutely nothing to stop her.

Enrique has billions. He lives in a three-story penthouse situated on Brickell Avenue, with unobstructed three-hundred-and-sixty-degree views of Miami and beyond. He has an extensive luxury car and couture collection. He has a construction company that is thriving beyond measure, just like his charities. He has great friends, an amazing family, plus looks and a physique that even the most body-conscious would die for, but in reality, he has nothing without Kristie.

The trouble is, Enrique is an act first, think later type of guy, and tonight he did just that. He's been going through hell over the past few months and has been reacting in ways he wished he could stop and change; however, it would seem that was impossible. He tried, he really did, but something more powerful than him kept causing him to self-destruct; it was like he knew what he was doing and knew what he needed to do to stop, but he just couldn't find a way, and this is what has led him to this moment, a moment that he will regret for the rest of his life.

His sad blue eyes shift from the floor-to-ceiling windows with views of Biscayne Bay that are completely lost on him, to his cell as it sits on the glass desk in front of him. His phone has been lighting up over and over again, notifying him that he has calls, texts, and emails, which will most probably be work-related, but he hasn't noticed as he's been in a daze ever since Kristie left, Lord knows how long ago.

Feeling utterly broken and nauseous, as he looks at his cell, which keeps lighting up with more notifications, he considers calling Kristie to ask her to come back so they can talk and work things out, but something inside is stopping him. A force greater than him is holding him back, it's making him feel like his hands are tied behind his back, refraining him from even picking up his phone. He stares blankly at it as it lights up and vibrates over and over again; he can just about see the picture of him and Kristie on the screen beneath the sea of messages and emails.

He stays seated, looking just as devastated as he actually is. His eyes then shift from his cell to a photo of the two of them together on one of the boats just off The Keys; he's wearing nothing but bright pink swimming shorts and his tan, and she's wearing one of his favorite white bikinis and a blue floaty cover-up. Kristie looks stunning, as always. Her long brunette hair is flowing in the breeze as she smiles sweetly, wearing her silver aviator shades. Her golden, silky skin is glistening in the sun as it shines down from above. This photo was taken during happier times, times when things were so beautiful and carefree, back when it felt like their love was enough alone to weather any storm, but sadly, he has now come to realize that this is not the case.

Kristie is the most beautiful lady he has ever seen, and he was so proud to have her by his side. He fell in love with her the moment he laid eyes on her nearly four years ago, when she walked past the Cardozo Hotel on Ocean Drive, where he was sitting on the porch having coffee with his friend Leon. He casts his mind back to that day... she was wearing the same color blue as she is wearing in this picture: cobalt blue, a color he adores on her.

At the time, he wasn't looking for anybody, he was happy alone and living the bachelor lifestyle, a lifestyle that consisted of work, working out, and going out, but he had no interest in women; they were nothing but a distraction... and a negative one at that. Every time he got involved with a woman, his life would be a mess, so he steered clear of them, and life was easy... he liked his life that way.

Then, one hot May afternoon, Kristie Carrington walked past him and turned his world upside down. For months, he saw her all over Miami, but he was too scared to approach her; she was oblivious to the spell she put him under until one evening that September, fate worked her magic, and they finally met, and Kristie fell in love with Enrique during that very moment.

Life has been a dream ever since. They have been so happy, and their love has grown stronger and stronger with each day that passed, but Enrique's deep-rooted issues from long ago, his suppressed grief, have forced him into a dark place. For most of his life, he has learned to live with it by ignoring it; when it tried to rise to the surface, he would push it back down as far as he could, usually with copious amounts of alcohol and hours upon hours of work, but it got to a point where the darkness kept rearing its ugly head more and more, and it was becoming impossible to ignore. Situations would arise that would trigger Enrique, sending him back to a place of grief and pain, plus the anniversaries of his mom's death or her birthdays became harder and harder to deal with; it was almost like when he and Kristie moved to the next stage in their relationship and moved in together, he put himself under this immense pressure to share every aspect of himself with her, and this was something he found impossible to do.

The sad thing is that Kristie is the only person he has felt that he could finally open up to about this, and she was more than willing to be there for him. She did everything she could and more to be there for him, but he had no idea how to allow her. He became increasingly frustrated with himself for failing her, as he saw it, and slowly turned into somebody he really isn't; somebody who would cause arguments and was hell to be around. He became so contentious and, at times, cruel. He would shut down and push her away, not in a physical way, but emotionally. When she tried to help him, when she showed him nothing but love and understanding, he would drive her away... he told her to leave, when she would tell him that she couldn't take anymore, and tonight, that is exactly what she did... she left... left him alone, with nothing but his own thoughts and feelings of heartache and regret.

He runs his hands through his perfectly styled jet-black hair, then over his unusually un-shaven face; he hasn't shaved in days, something that never happens... well, until these past few months. He's angry, angry with himself... angry that he didn't go after her, tell her that he loves her and wants her to stay... but what's the use when he can't do what it takes? Things will only go back to the way they were in a few days, weeks, or months, just like before. The only difference now is he could barely last a couple of days without slipping back into his self-destructive ways; she deserves better, she deserves to be free, free of his shit. Kristie has her whole life ahead of her... the world is her oyster, she's a strong and independent lady who doesn't need anybody to get on in life, and she most certainly doesn't need Enrique Cruz.

Kristie has and can make it on her own. When she met Enrique, she owned her own apartment and was expanding her spa to a larger property down at South Pointe Park, and now her spa has been named the best in Florida; people come from all over the country, some from abroad, for treatments at her facility due to her platinum reputation for Botox administration and so on. Kristie has a way of bringing out people's very best in the most natural of ways; she has developed a technique that truly is an art form, and people love what she does. Enrique's billions have never meant anything to her; she makes more than enough of her own.

Enrique knows he's been a fool to let her go, but he doesn't know what else to do. She deserves peace, not the tornado of hell he's been subjecting her to over the past few months. Yes, his stubborn Cuban nature was partly to blame; he got so angry with her at one point he really did mean it when he told her it was over, and when she went upstairs to pack her bags, in that moment, it was what he wanted, but deep down he knew he was just being childish and pathetic, there is no way he wanted any of this, he knew that then, and he sure as hell knows that now.

He glances back at the picture of the two of them again. To think that she is now in her apartment on South Beach, the apartment where they made so many happy memories: romantic dinners on the balcony over-looking the beach, lazy mornings spent in bed cuddled up or making love, days at the white sandy beach just in front of her building, it was such a perfect time in their lives. They would go out to dinner at one of the many restaurants nearby, wander around the neighborhood arm in arm, stopping for coffee at one of the cafés, sometimes Starbucks on Second Street, the very Starbucks where he saw Kristie for the second time in his life, the second time she knocked him off his feet.

He casts his mind back to that day as his eyes study her beauty; he remembers it like it was yesterday. He was having coffee with Freddie, his realtor, and everything stopped. He had been so blown away by her from the first time he saw her that he would look for this mysterious brunette everywhere he went, and suddenly, she crossed his path once more, sending him into a complete spin, not knowing which way was up.

Of course, Kristie had no idea, once again... she was just going about her day, getting on with what she needed to do, but Enrique was a mess. He completely zoned out and shifted his entire focus to Kristie, leaving a confused-looking Freddie wondering what on earth was going on. Somehow, he manages a smile at the memory, then all of a sudden, out of nowhere, he rises out of his chair with urgency; a hopeful thought has just shot into his mind... maybe she hasn't left... perhaps she's still here?

He rushes out of the office so fast he nearly sends his chair flying, then hurries to the foyer where the elevator is located, then he stops. As his eyes find the closed stainless-steel doors to the elevator in the empty foyer, he falls back onto the wall nearby; it's like all the oxygen has left his body... he can't breathe.

Unable to hold himself up, he slides down the wall, falling to the floor; she's gone... she's actually gone... and it's all my fault.

Chapter 2

After who knows how long, Enrique finds himself in a ball on the floor. Not having a clue how he got there, he finds just enough strength to lift himself up a little and sit upright with his back against the wall.

As he checks his devastating reality, his face feels wet. He reaches his hands to his face and touches it before pulling them away and looking at them with disbelief. Tears? Really? I've been crying? This doesn't seem real. Enrique hasn't cried since he was a child; he was six years old. When his mom passed, he cried a lot, and sadly, this got him an awful amount of attention. Members of the family would constantly ask him if he was OK and would rally around after him, so would teachers at school, etcetera. Enrique hated this; all he wanted to do was be the same as the rest of the kids. Yes, he only had one parent when all his school friends and the kids in his family all had two, but he hated the fact that he was always treated differently. Plus, he hated how he felt when he cried until one day, he forced the tears away, and the pain stopped, and so did the unwanted attention.

This has been his way of life ever since... Enrique doesn't cry, and sometimes, this has been to his detriment. When he and Kristie have discussed this during one of the rare times he has marginally opened up to her about this situation, they both wondered if he actually did cry, would it help him to become more open... would the words and feelings flow more easily? The trouble is, it's like since the day he forced the tears to stop, they all dried up and never came back, so he never got the chance to find out, although at times he felt like he was going to cry, but the tears would never fall... until now.

As he looks at his hands, he manages a sad chuckle, thinking how crazy life works sometimes. After everything, all the conversations and trying to find ways to help him release this anger and torment he has been carrying around with him for so long, it takes something as tragic as Kristie leaving for his body to finally release what it's been holding onto for all this time.

He cries and cries as he's forced to feel each and every emotion: loss, grief, despair, heartache, anger, love, frustration, self-disappointment, and most of all... self- hatred... he hates that he's the cause of the breakdown, of his relationship with Kristie, he hates that he was the one person that could have done something about it and so tragically couldn't. He's in excruciating pain... he's in agony, but there's nothing he can do to stop it. No amount of alcohol, working out, or time at the office will ease this pain... he has no choice but to face it, to deal with it... and he feels like absolute shit... he feels like he's dying.

All he wants right now is Kristie in his arms... to feel her close to him... to inhale her sweet scent as he holds her... to gaze into her eyes, and to lose himself in her like he has done so many times before. She is his remedy, his peace, his heart, and she's gone... he's finally driven her to leave him, just like she warned if he didn't sort out his shit. "There's only so many times you can say these things and retract them, Enrique... you can't keep doing this." Her words float through his mind as he sits, holding his legs close to him as he sits alone on the floor in the foyer of this very empty, and very sad penthouse. And she's right... he can't keep telling her it's over and then say he didn't mean it, without eventually pushing her to do exactly what he kept telling her to do... leave. He also couldn't keep treating her the way he was, leaving her alone night after night while he was either working, getting wasted, or picking fights with her, just so she would leave him alone and stop trying to help him face his demons.

As his tears finally subside, he feels strange... odd... he feels absolutely devastated and heartbroken, not to mention torn apart, but he also has this most strange feeling that he cannot describe or explain.

As he tries to figure out how he feels, he can't help but notice that he can breathe a little easier, it's almost like he feels relieved, like a weight has been lifted off his chest, but how can this be? How the hell can he feel relieved when he's just lost the most important person in his life... the only lady he has ever loved... there's no way he can be relieved, he's completely broken and destroyed over losing her, but he really does feel a sense of relief.

Shaking his head with disbelief, he musters the strength to get up. Dawn is breaking, and he would usually be getting up for his workout about now, but not today... in fact, he wonders if he will even go into work? That will be a first... Enrique Cruz, taking a day off sick... never! But perhaps today, he will?

Feeling confused by his sense of relief, as well as being absolutely heartbroken, he makes his way to the kitchen... he needs a drink. He pours himself some rum, filling the glass to the brim, drinks it down in one, then pours another before making his way out onto the balcony, carrying the glass in one hand and the bottle in his other.

As he sits in his chair overlooking the bay, the beauty of the colorful sky as the sun rises is lost on him; he can't shake this odd feeling. Yes, he can understand the heartache and pain, but this strange sense of relief is really throwing him. Then he wonders if it's something to do with him crying for the first time in nearly thirty years. Maybe that's what it is? Then he thinks that it's most probably because he's finally set Kristie free from him and his shit; she doesn't need to be dragged down by him any longer, she can now get on with her life... he's no good for her, and he's failed her so many times.

He sips his liquor, begging for it to take hold and numb out the pain, just like it has done so many times before. His eyes scan the bay, watching as fishermen come and go, others are making an early start on their journey to wherever their hearts desire; then suddenly, his eyes home in on Kristie's apartment building in the distance at South Pointe.

It's taking everything in his power not to go over there and beg for her forgiveness, tell her that this time it will be different, and make sure it really *will* be different... to follow through with his promises... but he knows it will never happen; he's incapable, incapable of giving her what she deserves. He really thought he could do it... he really thought he would find a way, but he couldn't seem to get a grip.

His eyes won't leave her apartment building, they are transfixed. Oddly, he feels a sense of comfort, it's giving him some kind of feeling of closeness to her, to know that he can see her home from where he is sitting... this is as close as he will get to her from now on, and he knows he will have to learn to accept this somehow.

His mind then wanders through thoughts of her being alone and upset, alone and upset, because of him. He knows that she is devastated; all she did was try to help him ease his pain, and all he did was cause it for her. She loved him in the most beautiful of ways, and he knows she still loves him, just like he still loves her, more than anything in the world; a love like this doesn't die, it's so special and pure, so sacred and unconditional, and this is why he has to let her go… because of how much he loves and adores her.

Thoughts of his mother enter his mind, and briefly, his eyes shift to the black and white photo of her on the glass side table just inside the door next to him. Not only does he feel like he's let Kristie down, he feels like he's let his mom down, too. He really does believe that his mom brought Kristie into his life to help him deal with his grief over losing her, but he couldn't seem to make it happen, he was too weak and too much of a fucking coward at that.

Deep down, he knows he caused arguments with Kristie to push her away, as she was trying to help him deal with things he found too difficult to face. He also knows that he stayed out late, either working or drinking, so he didn't have to come home and face her and any more of the conversations she was trying to have with him; conversations that would help him deal with his issues. It wasn't even like she kept on at him about it, but it was almost like, in his mind, he associated coming home and being around her, with the dread of these conversations, which really wasn't the case at all. He knows he made her life hell, and he didn't do enough to stop it.

As he contemplates life without his girl, the lady of his dreams… his love, his one and only true love, excruciating devastation explodes within him, ripping him to pieces. Then, all of a sudden, an avalanche of tears flood from his eyes, giving him no choice but to heave through them as they fall and fall, drenching his shirt as they roll uncontrollably down his face.

What the fuck have I done?

Chapter 3
Kristie

As Kristie enters her beautiful, contemporary apartment, a place she loved so much, a place she once called home and will do again, she wants to fall to the floor; she is devastated. Everywhere she looks, there are memories of her and Enrique; the day they looked at the apartment together, him checking out the standard of the workmanship, making sure it was up to code and to what was his idea of acceptable. The surge of excitement she felt when Luis, the realtor, showed her the closet and the view... oh, the view is magnificent, unobstructed vistas of Miami Beach, Downtown, and beyond; it really is a sight to behold.

Her heart falls to pieces once again, as she sees images of Enrique helping her move in and how elated he was for her that she achieved one of the major goals in her life, which was to move into this very building. She remembers the times they have cooked together in the kitchen right before her very eyes, as she stands in the entryway of her open-plan, all-white contemporary apartment. She can see them on the balcony having one of their many romantic dinners by candlelight as they listen to love songs and feed each other whatever delicious food they have cooked; it's like it was yesterday, but it wasn't... it was long ago, back when they could never imagine being in the situation, they're in now.

Heartbroken doesn't even come close to describing what Kristie is feeling right now, she really thought she would be with Enrique for the rest of her life. Who knows, maybe they will get back together, she can hope, but for that to become a reality, things will need to change. He will have to start facing things properly and deal with his issues, but until then, it just wouldn't be right to reconcile, it wouldn't be right for either of them.

Right now, Kristie has to protect her heart, and the only way she can do that is to be apart from Enrique, as painful as that is. She loves him dearly, she adores and worships him, and she knows he does her, too, but the past few months have been torturous hell for her, and she's pretty sure it has been for him, too. They couldn't carry on the way they were; it was destroying them both. She knows that if she had stayed much longer, they would have ended up in a more hostile place than they are now and would probably not even be left with as much as friendship. She hopes that they can still be in each other's life somehow, but for now, she thinks it's sensible to have a break from each other and give each other some time to breathe a little; things have been pretty difficult recently.

Taking a deep breath, she pulls her suitcase behind her and makes her way to the bedroom, then the closet, where she reluctantly begins to unpack her bag. Tears stream down her pretty face as she tries to comprehend what has just happened; has she really just left the love of her life... her world, her universe, her forever, her handsome Cuban, as she so fondly called him. How did this happen? How did things get so out of hand that she is now unpacking a suitcase full of things in her old apartment, a place she was going to put up for rent not so long ago?

She puts her skincare away in the bathroom and checks that she has everything she needs for the evening and the morning, if not, she will have to pop to the store and pick up some essentials, but for now, she thinks she will be OK. Thankfully, she had a housekeeper come to the apartment once a week to keep the place clean and fresh while she was living with Enrique and deciding what to do with her apartment. She also left some furniture there that didn't really have a place at the penthouse, so at least she has a sofa and a bed, plus some other items; more tears flood from her eyes as she thinks about how she's going to get the rest of her stuff from Alta Vita. "Ugh, God, I don't know." She whispers to herself, as she wipes her tears. "I have no clue... I guess I will figure it out in the morning."

She walks into the bedroom and looks at the bed, which is neatly dressed in white linens. She always had the bed made, as she and Enrique would sometimes stop by and stay over if they were out on South Beach. Her heart sinks as she thinks about the last time she was here; they had just been out to dinner at Prime 112 and had a little too much champagne. At the end of the night, they ended up here, at her apartment, and made love until the early hours. She feels devastated as she thinks of the intense connection they had, the love they shared and still share... it's a love like no other, a love she has never felt before... a love that will last until the end of time.

Completely heartbroken, Kristie walks over to the bed and falls down onto it with her face in her hands, and cries and cries. Her entire body is shaking as she tries to make sense of what's just happened, and how on earth she's going to face a future without Enrique.

* * *

With zero sleep, Kristie heads into work early before any clients get there; she's going to cancel all of her appointments for today and Wednesday. She needs to be on her a-game, and right now, she's far from that... she's a mess, and she wouldn't do her clients justice if she were to work over the next couple of days.

With her hair tied in a bun and minimal make-up, she discusses things with Colette and Mimi, but nothing on a personal level, purely professional. "I have a bit of a crisis going on." She explains. "It's personal... but I would never do this if I didn't have to."

"We know that, babe," Colette says, full of compassion, in her chic French accent.

"Just let us know if there's anything we can do," Mimi adds. "We'll hold everything down until you're ready to come back."

"Exactly," Colette says. "Take your time, babe... if you need anything... we're here... just like you've always been there for us." She smiles.

"Thank you, ladies," Kristie says with sadness. "It means the world to me... it really does."

She hugs them both and makes her way back up to her apartment without being seen by anybody else... thank God!

As she arrives back in her empty apartment, she makes her way out to the balcony and takes in the view for a few moments, breathing in the refreshing sea air, desperate for it to clear her mind and make her feel better... but she knows that it's going to take a whole lot more than a pretty view, and some sea air to make her feel better right now... even if it is the view that made her want to buy this apartment in the first place... a view she's always dreamed of waking up to every day. As she leans on the railings, she looks out up the tropical beach... her mind is blank... she feels numb... she has no idea what to do next... she knows what she has to do... but she doesn't feel like she has the energy or the brainpower to deal with it.

As she watches the aquamarine ocean lap against the powder white shoreline, she lets nature work her magic and give her the strength to face what she knows she's going to have to do today. Her eyes follow the crystal-clear water as it pulls back from the shore, then gently crashes back, over and over again, at a peaceful rhythm. The ocean has always had a positive impact on Kristie, and right now, she's holding onto the hope that it will do the same for her again.

She closes her eyes for a few seconds before opening them again, trying to calm her racing, broken heart. Anxiety blooms in her chest as she contemplates how she's going to contact Enrique about getting the rest of her things, but on top of it all, she's dreading telling her parents... they will be devastated, and she knows it will break her heart to go over it all once again, but also, the thought of moving out of the penthouse, a place she loved to live with the man of her dreams... the love of her life... it's crippling her with pain and grief. She never thought they would get here... ever.

It's true, it did cross her mind several times toward the end, even to the point that during one argument, one of many, she told him that if she leaves again, she would move back to her apartment for good... maybe she kept it for a reason. Of course, she said this out of anger and frustration, as Enrique was being his usual argumentative and mean self and told her to leave once again. She knew it was bad toward the end, but having said that, she still had hope that they would work things out some way... she could still see herself staying with Enrique for the rest of her life, but sadly, it just wasn't meant to be.

After a short while, her eyes shift from the shoreline out to the open ocean. As she takes in the view of the horizon, she takes in a deep breath and closes her eyes for a second before opening them once again. "You got this, babe." She whispers to herself. "You got this."

And with that, she walks back into her apartment and finds her cell.

As she holds her phone, her hands begin to shake a little, not because she's scared, but because she is heartbroken that she's found herself in this position... but as much as she doesn't want this, she doesn't have a choice; she has to do this.

Her thumbs begin to text a message she never thought she would ever have to write.

Hey,
I think I'll be able to
collect my things tomorrow.
Please let me know if this
is OK with you. Also, please can
I ask that you're not there?

Taking another deep breath, she closes her eyes and hits send. There's no point in delaying this, the sooner she gets this over with, the better… then she can begin her journey to healing from this devastating situation.

Enrique texts back almost immediately.

This is still your home.
You don't even need to ask to come here.
xxxxx

As she reads the messages, tears flood from her eyes. Just by reading his message, she knows he's hurting, but there's nothing she can do to help him, and as much as it kills her, she has to let go of trying.

She thinks about what to say back to him and then realizes it's best not to respond; she doesn't want to open up a conversation with him, plus she has no clue what to say.

Exiting the conversation, she then finds her mom's number in her call log and makes the gut-wrenching call she knows she has to make; she might as well get both of these conversations out of the way now, so it's done, and she doesn't have to think about it too much.

* * *

Wednesday, April 4th, 2018

As she stands in the foyer of the penthouse, Kristie's eyes sweep the beautiful space that she once called home. With her parents on either side of her, her mom puts her arm over her shoulders and comforts her as she tries to accept what she is about to do... leave her dream behind... her fairytale romance with her prince charming... the love of her life... this is it... the end... the devastating finale to her blissful, yet tragic love story.

"We're here for you, love," Vivian says to her daughter as she kisses her cheek. "Take as long as you need... we're here to help you through this, every step of the way."

Kristie nods, trying desperately to hold back the tears and stay strong... she has to... she has to be strong to get through this. "I think I just want to get it over with, mom." She says with a whisper, as anxiety tries to consume her. "I need to get my things and go... just being here... in what used to be my home with Enrique... up until a couple of days ago... it's too painful to even be standing here... amongst all our things... our dreams and our plans for our future... it's too much... I just need to get my things and go."

"OK, love... we'll help you do this quickly." Viv says.

"Where shall I start?" Jon asks sweetly; he feels for his daughter, he really does, and it's breaking his heart to see her this way... and it's also breaking his heart to have to do this... he really hoped that her and Enrique would be together forever... they seemed like a match made in heaven

"I'm gonna leave the furniture we bought together." She says, taking control of the situation... in fact, she almost sounds professional, like she's at work organizing things... but this is her way of coping, as she tries to push herself through this very sad and somber situation, she's found herself in. "I'm just going to take what I brought with me... there's my make-up table upstairs and a couple of chairs in the bedroom... plus that side table." She points to the table. "Also, gran and grandad's mirror... and some pieces of art... I'll show you them when we've got the furniture out... the make-up table will be heavy as it's mirrored... so we might need some help with that... maybe one of the doormen can help us?"

"OK, darling... I'll get started," Jon says, he walks to the phone, calls the doorman, and asks if somebody can help him carry some of the furniture.

"I need to pack my clothes and shoes... plus, my make-up," Kristie says.

"OK, darling... I'll help you with that," Vivian says.

In the closet, as Kristie and Vivian pack up the clothes and shoes, Kristie picks up the picture of her grandparents; they're leaning up against the light blue Thunderbird that is now in her mom's possession. She manages a tiny smile as she takes in the glamourous scene of her very elegant grandparents.

"I wonder what granny would say about all this?" She says, sounding just as devastated as she is.

Viv walks over to her daughter and puts her arm around her. "Well, darling, one thing's for sure... she would be very proud of you." She smiles. "You stuck it out... you tried so hard... you did more than anybody would have ever done, to make this work... you stood by Enrique through it all... but at the end of the day... you couldn't continue the way you were for much longer... Lord knows where you would be if you did... it was destructive and toxic... and there's only so long you can live that way without it having a devastating impact on you... an impact that could stay with you for the rest of your life."

Kristie nods in agreement.

"You're doing the right thing, darling," Vivian says with reassurance.

"Oh, mom." Kristie bursts into tears. It's too much for her. How did she end up in this situation? How did she end up here... in the home she shared with Enrique, packing up her things? How did this get so out of hand?

"I know, love, I know," Vivian whispers, as she glides her hand over Kristie's glossy brunette hair. "It's all gonna be just fine, though... it will all be OK... I just know it will... you have us... me and your dad... you have some amazing friends... everything will be alright... it might not seem it now... but it will... you're so strong and tenacious... you'll get through this."

"It just hurts so much, mom... it really does."

"I know, darling... but in time... things will get easier... I know it will."

They hold each other for a while longer, and Kristie gathers herself, trying desperately to pull herself together so she can at least get through this torturous moment.

"I guess, I'd better get on and get this done," Kristie says. "The sooner we get this done... the sooner I can get out of here... it's torture being in here... with the way things are with me and Enrique now... it doesn't feel right... it feels awful... I can't stand it."

"I know, love," Viv says. "We're nearly done now."

After an hour or so, everything is packed and out of the penthouse. As Kristie goes to leave, she sees the black and white picture of Gina on the side table in the foyer; she bursts into tears once again.

"It will all be OK, love... these things have a way of working themselves out... just give it time," Viv says softly. As she comforts her daughter, her heart breaks for her.

"I feel like I've let Gina down." Kristie sobs to her mom. "I promised her that I will take care of Enrique forever, that I will always be there for him."

"Just because you've left doesn't mean that you can't be there for him, darling," Vivian says. "But it wasn't good for you to stay with Enrique at this precise moment in time. He's a wonderful man who loves you very much, but his behavior was destroying you; he was making your life hell, and you were right to leave... but you never know what will happen in the future... I'm sure he will come to his senses and find a way to deal with his problems, but darling, until then, it's not healthy for you to stay... and Gina will understand that... I know she will... you can't stay because of something you promised his mom if it's destroying you, now, can you?"

"I know, mom, I know," Kristie manages, through her tears. "But it hurts like hell... I just wish none of this ever happened and I was here with him... but I'm not... I'm in my old apartment, alone... without him... the love of my life."

"I know, darling... but it's for the best... like I said earlier... it might not seem it now... but you'll see it in time... and you can always stay with us... you don't have to be alone."

"Thanks, mom... but I guess I will have to try to learn to live by myself again... and it's closer to work, too."

"OK, darling... but the offer's always there... you know that... or I can come stay with you... you know how much I love your apartment... although I would rather stay there under different circumstances."

"I know, mom... thanks... but I really should try to figure this out by myself."

"Everything's in the truck," Jon says, as he steps out of the elevator, not meaning to interrupt Kristie and Vivian. "We're all set."

"Thanks, dad," Kristie replies. She looks at Gina's photo one last time and apologizes to her in her mind... she's devastated that she couldn't be the one that helped Enrique out of his darkness and into the light. She really thought she could do it... but it breaks her heart to think that she wasn't enough.

With both of her parent's arms around her, she slowly walks toward the elevator, forcing her feet to step forward, as she feels like she's about to stumble and fall. Is this really happening? Is this real? Is this a nightmare? Is she really living through this moment... a moment that is hell on earth... so devastatingly painful she feels like she's dying inside? She tells herself that she's going to wake up any second and find out that this is a bad dream... but it's not... it's not a bad dream... this is very real... this is happening right now... and somehow, she's going to have to find a way to live with it, as she has no other choice.

The fairytale is well and truly over.

Chapter 4
Enrique

Aside from Kristie texting Enrique about collecting her things, they haven't had any contact, and it's killing them both; Enrique is going out of his mind, not being able to speak to her.

It's approaching midnight, and he is just walking through the door of the penthouse. It's taken him until now to find the courage to face coming home. After being greeted with the devastating sight of empty spaces where Kristie's things have been removed, the first thing he does is head straight to the kitchen and find his favorite bottle of rum and a crystal tumbler, which he fills to the brim. Running on nothing but coffee, way too many cigars, and most definitely way too much rum, he doesn't give it a second thought as he downs the whole glass, ready for another immediately. He fills his glass again and then heads out to the balcony, where he sits and drinks his liquor. He finds a cigar in the wooden humidor sitting on the table next to him and begins to prepare and light it. As he inhales the smooth smoke into his mouth, then exhales it, his eyes find Kristie's apartment building; he sits and looks out across the bay, wondering if she's OK. He so desperately wants to contact her, to call her, to hear her voice, but is it appropriate, and more importantly, would she even want to speak to him?

When she texted him yesterday about coming to get the rest of her stuff, he desperately hoped that it was a text to say she wanted to reconcile, but that would be wishful thinking on his part. He remembers being scared to open the message; sitting at his desk with his thumb hovering over the text icon, not knowing if he wants to read it or not. Unfortunately, it was a message he really didn't want to read.

Ever since the night she left, he's wanted nothing more than to message her to ask her to come home, but he knows it's no use. This is for the best... not for him, but for her, and he has to do what's best for her, as he loves this lady so much, and all he wants is for her to be happy, and sadly, that is something he can't seem to achieve.

As he sits sipping his rum, smoking his cigar, and gazing out over the bay at Kristie's apartment building, he wonders if he should text her, not to ask for her to come back home, but just to check on her. It doesn't feel right not having any contact with her, aside from practical exchanges... this is the love of his life, his soul mate, he will always want to know how she is and check in on her; just because they're not together anymore, why shouldn't they talk about their days and tell each other how they're getting on?

He reaches to the inside pocket of his blazer jacket and retrieves his cell. As he lights up the screen, he sees the picture of the two of them on the first night they met; he set this up on his phone the moment Kristie sent it to him, only days after they met. Her friend Lisa took it that night when they didn't even know she was taking the picture; he doesn't want to remove the photo, he loves this picture and doesn't know if he will ever remove it from his phone.

Then he notices the time displayed on the screen and realizes it's too late to text. Not exactly being on the ball, has led him to lose track of time and not realize how late it is. He decides he will text her in the morning at a more reasonable hour just to see how she is.

Putting his cell back in his pocket, he downs the rest of his rum and pours another. He's gonna need plenty of liquor to help him face going upstairs to try to sleep alone once again, and tonight will be even harder as he knows that all of Kristie's things have now gone, something he thought he would never see.

To Enrique, this house is just as much hers as it is his, and it always will be. Originally, he built this penthouse with himself in mind, but he met Kristie not long after the building was well underway to being constructed, and he decided to make it a home for the both of them, even though, at the time, Kristie had said she wanted to move into her own apartment on South Pointe and achieve her own goals before they made that kind of commitment. Enrique was happy to agree and waited for her to be ready. She moved in a year ago, in January, and they've been so happy living together until the last few months, when he seemed hell-bent on destroying things, until he finally pushed her too far, and she left; a tragedy he will never, ever get over.

* * *

The following morning

Enrique wakes from what must have been no more than an hour of sleep. Somehow, he found his way to bed, he's not sure how or what time, but he's woken to find himself holding Kristie's pillow. For a second, he thought it was Kristie... he was holding her pillow, and it smells of her... her very unique, sweet scent, laced with Coco Chanel, but to his devastation, she wasn't there; she's moved out, and yesterday, she took all her things.

He lies recounting the recent events, tortured by loneliness and regret... here he is, alone... alone in this huge bed, in this most spectacular penthouse, with nothing but memories of what he once had... such a perfect love story.... a perfect love story he got to live, until he destroyed it all.

He grips onto the pillow tighter, inhaling Kristie's scent, closing his eyes as he does; if only she were here, with him, holding him back, gazing at him with a look in her eyes that she can only give him, loving him in the way only she can. How he wishes he could still have moments like that, moments he's been privileged enough to experience for over three years, and now, it's almost like she's gone without a trace.

He opens his eyes for a second, and he notices something black underneath the pillow; it's one of her silk nightdresses. In a strange way, he feels relief in his heart... he still has something of hers. He reaches for the nightdress and holds it to his face with both hands, taking in a deep breath as he does, closing his eyes at the same time. For a second, it feels like she's right there with him, but as he opens his eyes, his reality hits him hard: she's not there with him at all, she's moved out... she's left him because of him, and his destructive behavior.

Placing the black silky garment down on the luxury sheets, he tells himself that there's only one thing he can do... *work*... get up, and go to work... take his mind off of this pain... this torture and torment... aside from alcohol and working out, his work is the only other thing he has found that helps him when his mind is screaming at him the way it is right now... but the only trouble is, right now, he doesn't just have his dark thoughts to contend with... he also has a broken heart to try and mend, and he has even less of a clue how to deal with that, compared to his darkness... all he can do is run from this as fast as he can... and that's exactly what he's going to do!

Feeling like absolute shit, he forces himself out of bed and makes his way to the bathroom; first, he needs a shower to freshen up, then he will call his driver, Emilio, and arrange for him to drive him to the office today; although he feels sober, the chances are, he's over the limit still, and there's no way he's going to take any risks in that respect... he feels very strongly about that.

As he makes his way to the bathroom, he walks through the closet for the first time since Kristie has taken her things; he's winded... he feels like all the oxygen has just left his body once again. Tears fill his eyes, and his heart breaks into a million pieces once more as he stares at the empty space where all her beautiful dresses and shoes used to be so neatly displayed. This really shakes him... since Kristie left, he's been in an even worse place than ever before, but for some reason, this has really set him on an even more devastating path of heartache. He knew that the closet would have been emptied of her clothes and shoes, but to see it, in reality, is a completely different story.

His mind replays some of the many times they have got dressed in here together, ready for a night out, a gala, or work. The times she has asked his opinion on an outfit... the times he walked in on her wearing nothing but her beautiful lingerie... the times they have made love in here. In his mind, he has a flashback to one of the times when he had just had a shower and walked into the closet to find her wearing one of his favorite white lingerie sets and Louboutin heels... he picked her up, carried her to the wall and made intensely, passionate love to her, as she gripped onto him, biting into his shoulder and moaning with pleasure. He shakes his head... Christ, did they have an intense love for each other... they loved each other hard... it was, and still is, a love that is not only so pure and so profound, it is also so deep and insanely raw... the passion between them was undeniable, and they couldn't get enough of each other... Kristie used to say that they could make love day and night and still want more... their need for each other will never be satisfied... and she was right!

Enrique can feel himself getting aroused as he thinks of him and Kristie; how can this be? He feels like death, but within a few seconds of thinking about making love to Kristie, he's feeling this way? But isn't that always the way, with Kristie Carrington, he tells himself. I never could get enough of her... why would things be any different now? The only thing that *is* different is that I can't be that way with her again... she doesn't even want to be around me, to the point where she asked me not to be here when she moved her stuff out. He shakes his head once more... he can't believe that this is the way things have turned out. He always thought they would be together forever... she would be his wife... and the fact of the matter is, she would have been, but Enrique couldn't seem to get his act together and drove her away. He tells himself that he knows what he needs to do to bring her back... he could try to work out this mess... but as great as that sounds, he knows that he can't do what it takes, and that is what makes him stay away, as it's not fair on Kristie to keep putting her through this. He has to do the right thing for her... and the right thing is that he stay well away from her, giving her the chance to heal and move on. She deserves to be truly happy and at peace... she doesn't deserve the hell he has put her through.

And with those thoughts in his mind, he takes a deep breath and heads to the bathroom, where he gets himself ready for another long day ahead of working relentlessly until he can't keep his eyes open; the only way he knows to deal with such torture.

Chapter 5
Friday, April 6th, 2018

Enrique has tried to message Kristie throughout the course of the week, but bottles it every time. Will she want to hear from me... after everything? Probably not, he tells himself. He misses her like crazy. He hates not having contact with her, but he's worried that he will be the last person she will want to hear from, so he leaves her in peace.

He keeps feeling these strange shifts inside of him today, and he's not sure what is going on with him. Amongst the sea of complicated emotions, he keeps feeling this odd sense of relief, and he's not sure why, as he knows he feels anything but relieved, he feels heartbroken and devastated, and there is absolutely nothing to be relieved about. He's so fucked up right now, he doesn't have a clue which way is up, so all he can do is wade through the swamp of hell he is drowning in.

When he feels out of control of his emotions, he sometimes finds that it helps to take a trip to the secluded beach he found years ago on Virginia Key; but there's no way he can even face going to the place that can help clear his mind, because it's so close to Kristie's apartment building. He worries that the closer he is to her right now, the more painful it will be; the fact that she would be so close, yet he can't see her, would be torture for him.

Right now, he feels it's best to avoid anything close to where Kristie is, especially South Pointe. Earlier today, a developer called and suggested they meet for lunch at Prime 112, which is down in the South of Fifth neighborhood, Kristie's neighborhood. He quickly came up with an alternative; there was no way he could risk running into her. As much as he would love nothing more than to see her, he also worries how he would feel if he did, especially in a professional setting. After all, she always goes to the Starbucks across the street from that very restaurant, so the chances of him seeing her are high, especially at lunchtime; luckily, he kept his vibe controlled and suggested meeting somewhere on Brickell or Downtown. He told the developer that he had another meeting afterward, and the traffic back across the bridge would make him late, no doubt. Thankfully, they didn't question it and agreed.

After they ask him over and over about what is going on with him, Enrique finally finds the strength to tell Sánchez and García about him and Kristie breaking up. He told Leon this morning while he stopped by for coffee; Leon is devastated for Enrique, but of course, Enrique did his best to put on a brave face in front of his friend. He is now at Panther Coffee with Sánchez and García, as he tries to get through another day of excruciating heartbreak.

"Look, papo, we're different breeds," Sánchez says. "You live your life so differently to us, and we respect each other's way of life... our differences... but we want you to know that we're here... here for you... like, seriously." He says, looking at García, then back to Enrique. "Me and Carlos feel that you might need someone to talk to... or not... like, whatever you need... we're here...."

"Yeah, papo... we're always here," García says. "Like, I know us guys are never good at talking about our shit, but you and Krissy... we know how much she meant to you... and even though you're apart right now... we know how much you still love her."

"Thanks, guys. But I'm OK, seriously." Enrique lies. "I guess it just wasn't meant to be... I mean, what else can I say?" He shrugs, as he leans on the table with his forearms. "I can't talk about it... and I won't...." He shakes his head as he has a flashback to him and Kristie sitting at the table next to where they're sitting, on the shaded terrace. They used to come here all the time. They used to sit out here watching the world go by, talking about anything and everything, with his arm draped over her shoulders as he kissed her. Sometimes, they'd get a takeout coffee and just wander around Wynwood and take in the scene of urban graffiti, with new galleries springing up here and there. They used to love coming here. He looks back at his friends through his blue mirrored aviators. "It kills me, it really does... but I can't do what I need to do... my shit just keeps getting in the way." He pauses for a second, letting out a long, slow breath. "And that's all folks." He says, looking just as devastated as he is. He then takes a sip of his cortado, looking away from his friends, trying to contain himself.

They both know exactly what he's talking about. They've been friends since school, and they know what he's been through, but they also respect that he doesn't feel comfortable talking about it. They just become his drinking partners when things get rough, while trying to keep an eye on him at the same time.

"Look, papo... I don't want to speak out of turn here... and please tell me to fuck the hell off if I'm crossing the line." Sánchez says, carefully and quietly, aware that they're in a public place, although away from everybody. He lights a cigarette, taking a sharp inhale, before exhaling the smoke, regarding his friend at the same time; he knows Enrique doesn't do well with talking about his feelings, but he's got to try and help somehow.

"No, it's OK... go on." Enrique says expectantly.

"Well... your grief... losing your mamá... has always been the driving force behind your hustle," Sánchez says quietly, keeping the conversation as private as it needs to be. He puffs some more on his cigarette, then takes a sip of his coffee, happy that Enrique hasn't told him to fuck off yet. "Money's never been your motive when it comes to your work... to your success... it's always been about helping people... plus, you've worked tirelessly to make your father proud and to show him that you buying the company from him was his best decision yet... and you've more than achieved that." He smiles. "But most of all, what's driven you more than anything... not just professionally... but in life in general... is making your mamá proud... I know that... I can see that." He says, hoping that he's making sense. "I guess what I'm trying to say is, as shitty as it is to carry this pain... it can sometimes be a blessing as well, as a curse... but the trouble is, it can eat you alive... and we have to find a way to ease that pressure... it's like a pressure cooker... if you don't twist the valve... it will explode fucking everywhere... and that's what keeps happening here... with you and Krissy... you don't have to say anything to us... we can see it... we have done for a while... and we want you to know that we understand... we might be from two different worlds, relationships aren't our thing... but we understand what's happening... we just didn't say anything, as we didn't want to interfere... we tried to check in with you a few times... but you didn't seem ready to discuss it... but papo... you're here now... talking to us... and I have faith... faith in God that you will get a handle on things... sometimes things have to get so fucking rock bottom... so fucking bad... catastrophic, even... before you can fix them... before you can make the changes you need to make... and we know that you'll fix it... you'll work things out... it's just finding what you're comfortable doing... to release that pressure."

"Exactly," García says, looking all sharp and elegant, dressed in his formal Bohemian attire. "Your work has always been super important to you... but you've always had trouble leaving the office... or the site... you have to have some time for yourself... you have to let yourself relax a little... and when I say time for you... I mean, actually, for *you*... you can't keep working yourself into the ground to avoid your problems... it's not healthy... we have to figure something out."

"I agree... we do need to figure something out because you're gonna get Krissy back... and we're gonna help you find a way...."

"Thanks, guys... but I don't know... it's all so fucked up... like, ugh... I just don't know." He says, shaking his head, before taking a sip of his coffee. He can't even put his words into order... he has no clue what to say. He loves his friends for offering their help and advice, but he has no clue what they can do to help him... he has no idea how to help himself with this situation, let alone how anybody else can help him. All he wants is Kristie back, but right now, he knows that's not a possibility, and it's killing him inside. Every second that goes by, another piece of him dies, and all he can do is let it happen. "The only thing that will help me, for now, is to get the fuck out on the town and forget about fucking everything for a few hours." He says with conviction.

"Then, that's what we'll do, papo," García says.

"I'm with you." Sánchez agrees.

"Perfect," Enrique says, managing a smile.

And with that, they all go out and get wasted all weekend. They end up in a gentleman's club, and a stripper tries to give Enrique a dance, and he declines; he's not interested. He might be wasted, but he's still deeply in love with Kristie, plus he's never been into this kind of thing. He's only here because it's where his friends want to be, and he doesn't want to go home back to an empty penthouse once again... he can't face it... so he'll stay out for as long as the night lives on!

* * *

Sunday, April 8th, 2018
Kristie

Following the most difficult week of her life, Kristie is spending the day at the beach with her friends, Lisa, Felicity, and Mario. She has worked super hard to catch up with the clients she had to cancel and is exhausted, but it meant so much to her to reschedule as soon as possible.

Kristie's friends have arranged a picnic on the beach to try to cheer her up and give her some company during this difficult time. Mario has been away working in Orlando, and Kristie hasn't told him yet, as she didn't want him to worry while he was working on such an important event.

As he arrives at the beach, he's all Gucci'd up and full of Italian flamboyance. He walks up behind Kristie and hugs her, then kisses her on the cheek and says, "I hear Mr. Cruz had one too many last night." As Kristie turns to face him, he can see straight away that something is wrong. "Oh, my darling... mi bella... what's wrong? What's happened?" He says, with deep concern, kneeling beside her with his arm over her delicate shoulders.

Lisa and Felicity both look up at him with sadness.

"Ladies, what's going on?" He asks, with his handsome face full of pain for his beloved friend. "What's happened?"

"Enrique and me have been having some problems lately." Kristie begins. "And well...." She bursts into tears.

"Oh, no... my darling... no." He folds her into his arms as tears fill his eyes; he can't stand to see her this way. "No."

Kristie nods as she cries in her friend's arms.

"Oh, baby girl, no," Mario says. "Oh, Bella... please, don't cry." They separate slightly, and Mario looks at Kristie. He puts his round Gucci sunglasses on top of his head, looks deeply into her eyes, and says. "You will get back together... you will work things out."

"I don't know," Kristie says. "I don't know if we will, Mario... he's just so... I don't know... shut down?" She explains. "He's so hurt and angry... he lives with this anger, and I can't help him... there's nothing I can do to help... things have just been so difficult recently... and finally I couldn't take anymore... things just got worse and worse." She swallows, trying to gather herself, before continuing. "I tried... I really did." She whispers.

"I know you did, my darling," Mario says with certainty. This is the first Mario has heard about this in any detail, as Kristie is so discreet when it comes to her relationship with Enrique. He knew that they were having problems, but not to this magnitude. "I know you would have done anything and everything to make things work." He continues. "I know that... but you two are meant for each other.... you're meant to be together... this is only temporary...."

Lisa and Felicity both agree.

"You'll work things out, babe," Lisa says with deep meaning, reaching for her hand and squeezing it. "I just know it."

Kristie nods; but as she agrees, she can't help but feel that this is the end for them. She can't see

Enrique ever going to a therapist, he's so against it, he doesn't want to talk to anybody else, even his father, and she doesn't feel like she's able to help him, as she feels like she has tried everything; she's at a loss with what to do. Then she remembers what Mario said to her when he first got to the beach; her entire being fills with concern and dread... she has to know what happened and if he's OK. "So, he was out this weekend?" She asks Mario.

"Um, yes," Mario replies, wishing he hadn't said anything now. One of his friends saw Enrique and his friends out last night, and Enrique was so drunk he could barely stand, but he will now do everything he can to water it down, as he doesn't want to upset Kristie anymore. He knows that this is probably Enrique's way of dealing with this... he just needs a blowout to get it all out of his system. "He was just a little drunk, ya know... had a few drinks," Mario says in a casual fashion.

"What do you mean?" Kristie asks, full of deep concern; she hates to think of Enrique in this kind of state without her being there to help him, and make sure he's OK.

"Oh, darling... it was nothing major... he was just out letting off some steam... ya know," Mario says.

"Where was he?" Kristie asks.

"On South Beach somewhere... one of the clubs, I think... he was with Carlos and Rico." Mario's tone is still casual, as he tries to sound vague as he gives as little detail as possible.

"Oh, I see," Kristie replies. She's worried about Enrique. She knows more than anybody that when things get too much for him, one of the first things he does is hit the bottle... hard... and she's scared that he's overdoing it. She decides to send him a text once she gets a moment alone. She has to check that he's OK.

The friends have their picnic on the beach and then have a swim in the turquoise ocean, absorbing the comforting warmth of the sun's rays as they beam down on them from above. After a couple of hours, Kristie needs to use the bathroom. She makes her way up to the restrooms in her apartment building, which is just behind where they're sitting, and texts Enrique on the way.

Hey,
Just wanted to see how
you're doing?
I do worry.
Love Krissy.
xx

He texts her back almost immediately.

Hey, mi amor,
I'm doing OK.

I hope you are?
I worry about you, too,
but please don't worry
about me.
Love Enrique
xxxxx

Kristie smiles as she reads his text. It's bittersweet; she's happy that she's heard from him, but she's so sad that this is the way things are between them. She wouldn't usually have to text him to check he was OK after going out on a weekend, as she would know as she would be living with him. She shakes her head with disbelief, she still can't get her head around the fact that this is their relationship now, it just doesn't feel natural to her.

She uses the bathroom and makes her way back to the beach, texting him back as she walks through the pool area of her apartment building.

I will always worry
about you, Enrique.
xx

And I will always
worry about you,
my darling.
But, please, I
want you to know
that everything is OK.
xxxxx

He texts again straightaway.

I wanted to text sooner,
but I didn't know if
you would want to
hear from me.
xxxxx

She texts back.

I will always want to hear
from you.
xx

And she does. Kristie may have left Enrique, and she has needed these few days to let the dust settle a little, but she can't imagine not having him in her life. He's had such a positive impact on her life for the most part, why wouldn't she still want to have contact with him? They may not have made it as a couple, but they can still be friends.

As she walks across the sugar-white sand toward her friends, she thinks about how she feels about this. She looks out to the horizon, taking in the view of the aquamarine Atlantic; of course, she still wants contact with Enrique, but she doesn't think it's a good idea to see him. She takes a deep breath; she knows that seeing him won't be a good idea. If they see each other, especially now, she worries that their emotions will get the better of them, one way or another, be it positive or negative, she can't risk either.

As she approaches her friends, she manages a small smile as they greet her.

"You OK, babe?" Felicity asks, as she sees her dear friend. "Feel better for your little walk?"

"Yeah... thanks," Kristie says, with another small smile as she removes her cover-up and lays down on her sun lounger. She allows the burning hot late afternoon sun to massage her tired, aching body as she closes her eyes, feeling a tiny bit of peace in her heart after messaging Enrique. She might know that he went crazy this weekend, but it's good to speak to him and check in on him; at least for now, she can do this and know that he's OK.

She's not exactly over the moon about the fact that he was in the state that Mario tried so desperately to downplay earlier, but like Mario said, he was probably just letting off some steam; things will settle down, and she will make sure that she checks on him regularly. At the end of the day, she has to detach to a point, although she will always love and care for Enrique; he was, and still is, the love of her life, her only love, and their kind of love doesn't just dissolve because they've gone their separate ways. Yes, she misses him like crazy and wants to go back to him and make things work, but it's no use... it's not good for either of them. She has to stay strong, not just for herself ,but for Enrique, too.

* * *

That evening, following their day at the beach, Mario calls Kristie and suggests they arrange a girly day with face masks and champagne.

"We can watch old movies and talk, girlie talk." He says, brimming with his usual Italian exuberance. "Eat lots of junk food... and spend all day in our pink silk pjs...like old times... it's been so long... we've all been super busy... life has kind of got in the way." He says. "How about it, baby? It will make you feel better... you up for it?"

"You're a sweet man, you really are, baby," Kristie replies, with her voice full of sadness and gratitude; she's so grateful for her friends... they're the best... and Mario suggesting a girlie day full of champagne, beauty treatments, and old movies only makes her love him even more. "You can all come to mine if you like... I'll supply the Botox." She smiles.

"No, baby... I don't want you working... you need some *you* time... we will be pampering you, baby girl."

"No... it's OK... it's not work for me... I love doing it." She smiles, as she pours herself some of the Cuban espresso she's just made; since meeting Enrique, her regular morning cafécito turned into an all-day affair, and it would seem like it's a difficult habit to break. "That reminds me, I need to top mine up at some point." She says, as she walks into the bedroom. "I haven't even had the chance... I never seem to have the time... I'm long overdue." She says, as she looks at herself in the mirror on the wall in front of her, running her finger over the slightest of lines in between her eyebrows. "I need to catch Colette when she's free... that's the only problem... she's been super busy, too."

"You don't need it, baby... you look beautiful... absolutely beautiful."

"Thank you, Mario... but, you sure don't need it... but, you still want it." She manages a tiny giggle before turning serious again. "But this... this with me and Enrique, has put years on me... I know it has."

"No, darling, you look fabulous... you always do."

"Thanks, babe." Kristie smiles. "And so do you."

"You're so kind, Bella." Mario smiles. "So, let me know when you're free... and I will make sure Lis' and Flick are free, too... and we'll make it a date."

"Thanks, babe... you're the sweetest, you really are."

"Baby girl, that's what I'm here for... I want to help... I want to be there for you... please... if there's anything I can do... please tell me... and I'll be right there... even if you need me to just come sit with you... please don't sit alone... I will come over every night and day until you feel ready to be alone... I will do anything... anything... just say the word, my darling."

"Awww, Mario." Kristie begins to cry. "Thank you so much."

"Oh, Krissy, baby... please don't cry... please... aww... I hate this... please...." Mario's heart is broken for his dear friend.

"I'm sorry... it's just... I miss him so much... I hate this... all of this... I never wanted to leave... but I had no choice... I had no choice."

"I know, darling... but this is only temporary... believe me... I know... it's only temporary... you will be back together in no time... I just know it...."

"Thank you... but I don't know... I just... it's like, it's all I want... but I worry things have gone too far... I worry that he's too deep in his... I dunno... like, he's so far down this black hole... or whatever it is... like, will he ever be able to talk about this... and if we do get back together... will we always have to face these issues... his mood swings and lashing out... will this be the way things are?" Kristie is so insecure about everything right now... she's unsure of her whole life... nothing makes sense anymore, and she can't help but feel negative about everything.

"No, no, my darling... it won't be like that, at all... he will find a way, baby... he will... this is not forever... he will find a way... I just know it... and we'll all be celebrating your wedding in no time... please, baby... trust me... I know these things."

Kristie manages a tiny giggle.... a giggle of disbelief... she loves Mario for his optimism and for him trying to reassure her, but right now, in this moment, she can't see it happening.

"Honestly, my darling... have faith... it will happen... I just know it." Mario confirms.

"I love you for saying that, babe... I really do." Kristie replies through her tears.

"And I love you, Bella... now... would you like me to come over? We can watch Audrey or Marylin... whatever you want... Real Housewives... I'm up for anything... I want to be there for you."

"No... it's OK, babe... thank you, though... I'm super tired and could do with a hot bath and an early night...."

"OK, my darling... as long as you're sure."

"I'm positive."

"OK, well, have a think when you're ready for us bitches to come over and invade your space... and we'll be right there in a jiffy."

"I will, babe." Kristie smiles. "And thank you... thank you so much... it means the world to have friends like you."

"And it means the world to have friends like you, too."

They say their goodbyes, and Kristie walks out to the balcony and looks out to the horizon, trying to find some peace in her tortured heart and soul.

Chapter 6
Wednesday, April 11th, 2018
Enrique

Enrique feels comfort in the fact that he and Kristie are in contact. It might not be the same as before, but at least things are friendly, and they can catch up with each other.

Today marks one week since Kristie took her things, which is a sad day for Enrique as he allows himself a moment to think about it. He's been trying desperately not to dwell on things too much and get on with it, although his idea of getting on with it is working all the hours God sends, working out like a madman, and drinking to excess.

Later that evening, José comes to the penthouse, and Enrique finally tells his father about him and Kristie, keeping the details limited and asking him not to share his heartbreaking news with the rest of the family just yet; he's not ready to face them all asking questions etcetera at the moment.

"It's all my fault," Enrique admits, looking extremely disappointed in himself. "I fucked it all up with my shit." He says with frustration, taking a puff on his cigar as they sit up on the pool deck. "I just couldn't get a handle on things... and kept lashing out at her... destroyed the whole thing... destroyed everything... all she wanted to do was love me... love me and help me... and I treated her so terribly... abominably." He looks to his father and says. "You were right all along, papá... and I saw it too late... just like you warned... but I was too stubborn to see."

"It's not like that, papo... it's not about who's right or wrong... I'm just... I'm just so sorry." Tears fall from José's dark brown eyes as he listens to more of his son explaining what has happened; yes, he saw this happening, and he warned Enrique a few times, but he was in too deep... too wrapped up in his shit to listen... shit that *he* takes responsibility for, whether Enrique will accept that or not, is a different story, but José will always take the blame for the way Enrique has handled the death of his mother. "I'm absolutely devastated... devastated beyond belief... and I'm devastated for you both, too... God knows what you must be going through... and Krissy." He wipes his tears, still holding his cigar in one hand. "God, Enrique... I really hoped you could make it... I really did." He shakes his head with sadness. "I love Kristie like a daughter, and she will always be part of the family."

"I feel the very same," Enrique says, looking down with gut-wrenching heartache and shame... shame, because he destroyed it all... he couldn't make it work... he couldn't make it happen... he's let everybody down, himself, his father, his mother, their families, and especially Kristie.

To Enrique's relief, José doesn't lecture him with I told you so's, but he tells him that he needs to sort his shit out, and if he does, he will stand a good chance of getting her back.

"I've got to be honest, papá... I wonder if she will even want me back after the way I've treated her." Enrique says with sadness; he might feel like absolute crap, but somehow, he still looks sharp as anything in his black Armani suit and pink shirt.

"She will... I have faith that you will get back together." José says, raising his hand to the sky. "Faith in God... faith in you." He says with teary eyes, raising his eyebrows at his son.

They hold a long-extended gaze for a few moments; Enrique understands the meaning of the look in José's eyes... there is no need for words.

Enrique breaks their gaze and looks out to the bay before taking a puff on his cigar. Is there a chance they could work things out like his father is suggesting? Could he put things right? Make it all up to her... will she forgive him for all of his mistakes?

Then, reality doesn't take long to hit like a ton of bricks, and the wind is taken out of him within seconds... he would love to make it right with Kristie... but it's impossible, and he knows it.

* * *

Once José gets back to his home on Star Island, he texts Kristie as he stands in the stylish great room decorated in dark wood and cream.

I just want you to know how sorry I am.
I also want you to know that I love you
and you will always be like a daughter to me.
Please let me know if
there's anything I can do to help,
and if you feel comfortable with it,
I will always be here for you, cariño.

Kristie texts back.

Thank you, José, it
means so much to me, and
you will always be like a father to me.
I love you dearly, too.

José smiles when he receives the text back from Kristie. He puts his cell in the inside pocket of his jacket, then finds himself walking over to one of the many photos of his darling wife, Gina.

He picks up the beautiful photo of her and smiles at her before saying. "We need to get these two back together again, mi amor... our son is devastated... and I know Krissy is too... they belong together, and we need to help them... we need to help them find their way back to each other." Tears flood from his eyes as he studies the picture of the only lady he has, and will ever love. "Please, baby... help me, help our son."

As the tears fall from his eyes, he places the frame back down on the side table, finds his linen handkerchief in his pocket, and wipes away his tears. He needs a drink... he needs to go sit in his favorite chair at the dock, look out to the bay, and think... think about how he's going to help his son finally face what he's been running from for all these years, as he knows that if he can achieve that, Enrique will quit with the anger and mood swings, as well as put down the bottle for once, and deal with his issues once and for all.

He has to find a way... and he has to do this now. But will Enrique let him?

* * *

Since Kristie texted Enrique on Sunday, she and Enrique have talked on the phone every night, simply checking how each other is and talking about what they have been up to. Of course, Enrique will never reveal to Kristie just how excessive his drinking has become since she left; to be fair, he won't even admit to himself how bad he's been.

This is the longest they have been apart since they got together, and it's been hell. Following a difficult day at work, plus the conversation with his father, Enrique needed to talk to Kristie more than ever; even after all is said and done, Kristie is the one who he will always want to talk to when he's had a bad day... and even if he ever has a good day again, which he highly doubts now they're apart, but if he does, he will want to talk to her then... he will always want her in his life.

As 10:30 comes and goes, Kristie and Enrique are still texting; she had a late finish tonight and has just got through the door to her apartment... she's ready for a hot bath and her bed.

She continues to text him throughout her bath and while getting ready for bed.

Once she's in bed, Enrique texts;

Shall I call you?
It might be easier
than texting?
xxxxx

Kristie replies.

Of course.
xxxxx

Her cell rings, and she answers. "What you up to, babe?" She asks.

"Working... in the office at home." He says. "How about you?"

"Just got into bed... I'm so tired."

"Oh, baby... you do too much." Enrique replies sweetly.

"You can talk, Mr. Cruz... every time I speak to you... you're in the office."

"There's always something to do, baby." He says, like it's nothing... he knows she's got him... he knows that she knows, that he's doing his usual, and burying himself in his work to distract from his very painful reality.

"Babe... please take it easy... I know you're not sleeping... and all this work... I worry."

"It's OK... I'll be finished in a bit... just got a few things to tie up... then I'll have an early night." He manages a smile, knowing that Enrique Cruz and early nights don't mix... it will never happen.

"God, I miss you." She says with a whisper. The words escape her lips before she can stop them.

"I miss you, too... more than anything in the world." Enrique follows her lead... it's just so natural to him to tell her something like that... especially as he feels it more than ever, right now.

"Really?" She asks in a sweet voice.

"You know I do... you know I can't stand this... but I understand... I really do... things couldn't carry on the way they were... *I* couldn't carry on the way

I was… the way I was treating you… my behavior… it's abhorrent to me to even think of behaving that way toward you… you didn't deserve any of it, and you were right to leave." He reigns it in, as he has to be strong for both of them. The truth is, he's struggling more than anything, but he wants to try and not to show Kristie that he feels this way, as he doesn't want to make her feel any worse than she already does.

"I don't want any of this, either… I hate every second of being apart from you… being alone in this bed, without you… with all the memories we've made… it's so heartbreaking, Enrique." Kristie begins to get upset. "I want you here… holding me… kissing me… the way we used to."

"Oh, baby girl, I would love nothing more… to hold you in my arms… to take away all of this pain… to love you… to make everything right again…." He stops himself. "I'm so sorry, baby… I shouldn't have said that… it was inappropriate of me."

"No… no, it's OK… it's my fault for telling you that I'm in bed… I know what the two of us are like." She giggles. "I should know better."

"No, baby… *I* should know better… I should have diverted the conversation… I'm sorry… it was wrong of me… I love you… and I know we don't want to confuse things… I'm glad that we're talking… it's nice that we're in this position… that we can feel that it's OK to do this… as much as I'd rather you here... with me... I know that's not possible... but it's nice to know that we can still talk... that we can be friends."

As Kristie hears him say these words, her heart breaks... friends? To think of Enrique as anything other than her boyfriend... her partner, just doesn't feel right to her... as much as it's true... they are friends now... it's a bitter pill to swallow.

"You, OK, baby?" He asks with concern, as she's gone quiet.

"Yes." She says. "Yes, I'm OK." She manages a smile. "Just a little tired, that's all."

"OK, baby... well, as long as you're sure?"

"Yes, I'm sure." She says, trying to be as strong as she needs to be. All she wants to do is ask him to come over and make love to her... make everything right again, just like he said, but she knows that would be the wrong thing to do. She knows that nothing has changed, and things will go back to the way they were in no time, and she can't risk that. "I guess I'd better get some sleep, as I have an early morning ahead of me... plus, you need some rest too, baby."

"OK, baby." He pauses for a second before saying. "You sure you're OK?"

"I promise, babe." She replies cheerfully. "You're right... everything you said was right... and it is nice that we can still be friends."

"It is." He agrees. "I could never imagine you not being in my life... not ever."

"And I feel the very same, babe."

"Well, that's good to hear." He smiles. "I love you."

"I love you too." She says sweetly.

As they end their call, Enrique sits in his office, he thinks about Kristie there, all alone in her bed... alone when she could be with him... what a tragic situation he has created. Yes, he put on a front to protect her, he doesn't want to keep burdening her with how much he misses her and about how much pain he's in... he wants to be strong for her... he wants to be there for her.

As he sits and contemplates the situation, he tells himself to fix this mess... go see a therapist, and deal with his shit... but every time he thinks about it, he feels like he's going to throw up... the anxiety is suffocating... he feels like he wants to crawl out of his own skin... he can't bear it. The thought alone is intolerable; the whole situation is impossible, and who's to say that she will even want him back... yes, they're getting along, but he can't afford to take anything for granted as far as this mess is concerned... he fucked this up royally, and he will have to suffer the consequences... and suffer is what he is doing. She's better off without him anyway, he knows this, so he will have to learn to live with it.

Chapter 7
Saturday, April 14th, 2018

Kristie has just heard that Enrique has been out for the past two nights, falling out of clubs. As she sits at her desk during her lunch break, she feels a strong need to call him to check in, as she's worried; as much as she's trying not to get involved with his life, she can't help but worry… she still loves and cares for him just as much as she did when they were together.

She finds her cell and dials his number. As he answers the phone, she can hear that he's just woken up, and this concerns her even more; Enrique has always been one to be awake at the crack of dawn and in the gym before he can even think about it… this is so unlike him, well it was, until these last few months. "Enrique baby, please… this isn't healthy." She says, after they've exchanged pleasantries.

He says nothing as he lays in bed feeling like absolute shit and looking it too, with three-day's worth of stubble on his handsome, dark face… his exotic features are rugged at best, and his hair is all over the place.

"Enrique… please." She pleads with him, after briefly telling him what she's heard.

He lets out a long, slow breath… he really could do without this… his head is pounding, and he feels like death. "It's not true." He says simply.

"Enrique… please… I'm worried, that's all." She says.

"Look, I'm OK." He tells her in a firm tone. "As they say… believe none of what you hear, and only half of what you see… this *is* Miami, after all… people talk shit all the time."

"Enrique, don't patronize me," Kristie says in an agitated fashion. She cares about him and has reason to be concerned, after all, it is lunchtime, and he's still in bed… it's obvious that there's some truth in what she's heard, and she's tired of his attitude toward her when she shows concern for him. "It's coming from somewhere." She says.

"Yeah, people's minds… they're bored with their own lives, so they have to make shit up about mine!" He rants. He's in no mood for this, and quite frankly, he's had it! Why the fuck can't she give him a break? "Come on, Krissy, you know the drill… people talk shit all the time… and guess what? I don't give a fuck, what people are saying about me… at the end of the day, I don't give anything away, so that's why they have to make shit up… you've known this all along." Enrique knows this would usually be the case, as he's always been so discreet, but he knows in his heart that recently he's been more than careless, and he also knows there's some truth in what Kristie has heard; but he will never admit that.

Enrique absolutely hates that due to his status and charity work, he's known publicly around Miami and South Florida, and he wishes he could find a way not to be... but aside from what he's already doing, there's not much else he can do.

Judging by his reaction and the fact that he's so obviously still in bed at this hour, Kristie knows that there is truth in what she's heard, but she also knows there's no talking to him, so she backs off. "OK," she relents. "I just... I know we're not together anymore, but I still care."

"Well, perhaps you shouldn't." He snaps in Spanish, then hangs up on her.

He chucks his cell down on the bed beside him, closes his eyes, and covers them with the back of his forearm; his head feels like it's about to explode now after that! I'm no victim, he tells himself. I can take care of myself.... I don't need to be checked up on, or recused... I don't need to be rescued from shit! Who the hell is she to tell me what I can and can't do? *She* left me at the end of the day... why does she care about what I get up to? I went out for a few drinks, that's all... it's no big deal... Jesus!

Then, his cell vibrates on the bed next to him, making his head pound even more. He doesn't want to even move right now, but if he doesn't stop this vibrating sound, he's going to scream.

With his eyes still covered, he attempts to cancel the call but fails miserably, and it keeps vibrating and vibrating, over and over again... it feels like each ring is getting louder and louder. He forces himself to uncover his eyes and look at the screen, squinting his eyes as he does, telling himself that it will be Kristie... but it's not... it's his father... he has to answer.

"Hi." He says, in Spanish, with a gravelly voice.

"Enrique, papi, what's with all this chisme that's doing it's rounds all over town."

"What gossip?" Enrique acts like he doesn't know a thing about what his father is talking about. He covers his eyes with his forearm, shielding them from what little light is in the room... right now, he wishes he could shield himself from this conversation. The last thing he needs is a lecture from his father, too.

"You... falling out of clubs at 6am? Singing at the top of your lungs walking down Collins... Enrique... papi... come on... you've got to get a grip."

"Not you, as well," Enrique says dismissively.

"What do you mean?" José asks with confusion.

"Ugh… it doesn't matter. Just people talking shit… totally exaggerated, as always with this town."

"If that's the case, why does it sound like I've just woken you up?" José asks in a judgmental tone.

"Jesus Christ, dad, can't a guy have a few drinks?" Enrique's exasperated.

"Look, you're my son… I worry… you're really going through it… you're my responsibility." José says in a serious tone. "I'm not gonna stand by and watch you drink yourself stupid… not to mention let you make a fool of yourself around town."

"Dad. I'm fine. Please don't worry."

"I always will. It's my job. I worry about you."

"I'm fine. Don't worry. Please." Enrique says. "It's all bullshit."

"Hmm… well, I don't buy it… you've gotta take care of yourself, papi… do yourself a favor and put the bottle down… focus on your health and getting your head straight." José advises. "Why don't we go out on the boat tomorrow? Do some fishing… have some father and son time."

"I can't tomorrow, dad… I'm working… I'll try to come over in the evening, though."

"OK... well, if anything changes, let me know... I'm here, papo... I'm here for you... I wanna help... help you get through this...."

"I'm OK, dad... seriously."

"You keep telling yourself that... I know different... I know you have to get this out of your system... but please, Enrique... take care of yourself... it's no good, drinking that way...."

"I had a few drinks, dad... I tried to have a good time, that's all."

"OK." José relents; he knows he has to tread carefully as Enrique is just as stubborn as he is, so he knows he can't keep on at him. "I'll see you tomorrow night, all being well."

"Yes... see you tomorrow night... I'll let you know if I finish early."

"OK, papi... take care... and get some coffee and a good breakfast... lots of water," José says, letting his son know that he knows the rumors are most likely true.

"I will."

They say their goodbyes, and Enrique just about manages to look at his screen long enough to turn off the vibrate function and tries to go back to sleep. He's frustrated beyond belief; why the fuck can't people leave him alone? All he did was go out and have a few drinks? Why's it such a big deal? What's with all the phone calls and interfering?

Then, out of nowhere, his cell rings... it's so loud... ear piercing, in fact... Enrique feels like his head is about to explode.

"What the fuck!!!!!" He exclaims. "I put it on silent!!"

He scrambles for his cell and opens his eyes just enough so he can find the button to turn the fucking thing off. Fuck this! What's a guy gotta do to get some rest around here?

He holds the button down, and for the first time in his life, he actually turns his phone off. He's going to get some rest if it kills him!

* * *

Kristie
A few moments earlier

Kristie looks at her phone in disbelief... she's done it again, she's shown Enrique genuine concern, and she's been met with resistance, just like every other time. In this moment, she realizes that perhaps being friends with somebody who she shares such a deep love, yet has so many unsolved issues with might not run as smoothly as she fantasizes about. Maybe she's expecting too much from him and the situation… maybe she's being naïve to think they could make this work as a friendship? Things are too raw… too ripped open, and painful to expect anything else.

Tears fill her eyes as she imagines a life without any contact with Enrique, whatsoever… she doesn't know if she can face it, but she knew that this would probably be the case when she made the decision to leave. Maybe it's too soon… maybe this is something they will be able to revisit at a later stage once the dust has settled?

Leaving her lunch as she's not hungry anymore, she tries to pull herself together, ready for her next client. She has an afternoon full of appointments and then home for another night alone, crying herself to sleep, just like she has every single night since she left the love of her life.

* * *

Sunday, April 15th, 2018
Enrique

Enrique has to admit he feels terrible for the way things went down with Kristie yesterday. Once he'd calmed down and saw things for how they really were… Kristie showing him nothing but love and care, just like she always has done, he has felt an overwhelming need to apologize to her. But will she want to even speak to me, after the way I treated her yesterday, he asks himself.

81

After a short while contemplating what to do next, he decides there's only one way to find out… and that's to call her… a text simply won't do, he needs to call her and apologize for the way he acted… and he has to do it now.

He picks up his cell and makes the call.

"Hey." He says quietly, glad she picked up.

"Hey." She replies, sounding so down it breaks Enrique's heart.

"I'm so sorry, baby… I really am… you didn't deserve that… the way I acted… I need to do better… I'm so sorry, I really am… I know sorry isn't good enough… I know… but it's all I can do… apologize."

"It's OK," Kristie replies. It's not OK, but what else is she going to say? Although her head is telling her to sever all contact with Enrique right now, her heart won't let her… she misses him, and for the most part, she's enjoyed talking to him on the phone every evening.

"It's not OK, baby… certainly not by me… I was terrible to you… disgusting… and you don't need it… you were only showing your concern… not that there's anything to be concerned about… but I know what you were doing, and you didn't deserve me treating you that way... I love you, and I'm sorry... I can't apologize enough."

"That's all I was doing, babe... just checking in on you, as I was worried... but you're right... people talk... and I guess it's none of my business... I just worry that's all."

"I know you do, baby... but seriously... they're exaggerating... I was just out, that's all... not having a good time... but I was out, and I'd had a few drinks... nothing like what people are saying." He knows he's being economical with the truth, but he doesn't want her to worry, and if he's honest, he won't even admit to himself how bad his drinking is right now.

"Well, I do know how people talk." She says, deciding not to mention that it was obvious that he was still in bed at lunchtime... something that was always unheard of... but she wants to keep the peace. At the end of the day, he's a grown adult and can do as he pleases... they're not together anymore, so she has to learn to take a back seat when it comes to these kinds of things, although she knows it will be difficult as she cares about him so much; she knows that this is the only way he knows how to deal with things... so, she's sure things will calm down in time.

"They do, babe." He replies sweetly.

"So, does this mean we're back to being friends again?" She asks with a smile.

"That's if you'll have me?"

"I'll always have you." She giggles.

"Oh, baby… please… don't." He chuckles back. "You'll get me into trouble."

"Oh, no… this bad girl's on her best behavior." She giggles, trying to lighten the mood; she doesn't know where the hell that came from, but she's going to go with it… she's missed laughing, and she's sure missed flirting with Enrique.

He chuckles, loving that she's using a saying that he's said to her in the past, when they've been teasing each other… and he finds it as hot as hell. "Oh, Miss Carrington… I know from first-hand experience that that is *never* the case!"

They both enjoy the feeling of being back in their little bubble for a few moments… but they both know that it's going to burst any minute… as their reality is that they are no longer together… they are living separately because of Enrique and his shit… but for now… for this brief moment, they're going to bathe in this sweet sea of dreamy reminiscence, of what they once were.

Chapter 8
Saturday, April 21st, 2018

"Come on, babe... you're coming out with us," Lisa says to Kristie, as she walks into her oceanfront apartment dressed up to the nines. "Now, come on... let's get you out of these sweatpants and into some glad rags... girl, we're going for a night on the town!"

"But I really don't feel up to it, babe." Kristie pleads. She's removed all her make-up and has her glasses on, ready for a night in front of the TV watching Audrey Hepburn movies, with popcorn for her dinner.

"Babe... you never feel up to it... but once you're out... you'll have the time of your life... now... hop to it!" Lisa says in an upbeat tone. "Mario and Flick are on their way... so we need you glammed up, pronto!"

"But...." Kristie protests.

"No, buts... just, yes... let's go... come on, girl... get in that swanky closet of yours, and pick out something sparkly... beat that face with some wall paint... pull your hair out of that ponytail... and sling on some heels... I'll find the wine... get you in the mood a bit... maybe some vodka!"

The doorbell goes; it's Felicity and Mario.

"Hello… is this where the intervention is taking place?!" Mario hollers as he walks through the door, looking all Gucci'd up and raring to go.

Kristie smiles at her friends; she loves them so much for trying to help her out of her depression, and although the last thing she wants is to go out on the town… the fact that they have made the effort to come to her apartment and encourage her to leave this building for the first time in weeks, makes her love them even more than she already does.

* * *

All four friends go to a few bars around South Pointe, and then up to the bar at The Ritz Carlton, then onto another in Lincoln Road, where they decide to have a few drinks before making their way to Story, a club they have tickets for this evening; they're going to have a blast if it kills them… their sole purpose is to take Kristie's mind off of her break up with Enrique, and so far, they seem to be doing a great job!

Feeling a little tipsy on the two cocktails she's had, Kristie makes her way to the bathroom, leaving her friends at the table they're all sitting at in the salsa bar.

Once she's done what she's got to do in the bathroom, she washes her hands and checks herself in the mirror; she looks and feels like death, in her opinion, although her friends tell her otherwise. She checks her make-up as she dries her hands and decides to touch it up a little.

Once her make-up is as good as it will ever be, during a time like this... no sleep, hardly any food, and way too much stress, she then straightens her dress as she looks in the floor-length mirror; her dress is loose, just like all of her clothes... that's what happens when you don't eat for days at a time... but right now, she can't help it... she can't face food right now.

Finally, she takes a deep breath, picks up her purse from the vanity, and makes her way back to her friends. On her way back from the bathroom, she stands still for a second, figuring out where her friends are... she's a little out of sorts at the moment and keeps forgetting things... simple things like where she left her friends are becoming very regular for her, and it's as annoying as hell... but she has to give herself a break, as she is totally exhausted, and now, tipsy on the two cocktails she's had.

"I hear lover boy dumped you?" A voice whispers into her ear from behind her, nearly making her jump out of her skin, especially as it's a voice that sounds familiar.

Kristie turns urgently, looking shocked and disturbed once she sees who it is, confirming her suspicions. "Oh, go away, Peter." She snaps with an exasperated expression. Although the alcohol she's consumed has helped numb her pain to a certain extent, she still feels incredibly heartbroken, but she's going to make damn sure that Peter isn't going to see any of that.

"Ohh… touchy, aren't we?" He sings through his words as he moves so he's facing her. "Now he's out the way… perhaps we can pick up where we left off, ya know." He says, looking all smarmy and gross.

Kristie looks at him with complete disbelief. As if she would even consider getting back with him… she can't even stand to be in the same room as him, let alone be in a relationship with him. He repulses her to the point where she feels sick to even look at him; what on earth did she ever see in him?

"We were so good together." He continues, before reaching his hand up to her face.

Kristie slaps his hand away. "Don't touch me!" She snaps. "Don't you ever touch me!"

Security overhears Kristie telling Peter to leave her alone, and makes his way over to them. "Everything OK, ma'am?" The burly guard asks, looking ready to remove Peter any second now… all she has to do is say the word.

"Yes... thank you." Kristie says to the security man." Peter was just leaving." She says, looking at him with disgust.

"What's going on, babe?" Lisa says, as she notices what's happening and hurries over to Kristie with Mario and Flick beside her.

"Nothing," Kristie says calmly. "Peter was just leaving."

"Yeah... you should leave," Flick says, looking at him with disgust.

"Come on, my friend." The security man says, taking Peter by the arm. "It's time to leave."

"But we were only talking... that's all." Peter pleads. "Jeez, you can't even speak to somebody these days? What the hell is going on with this world?" He says, trying to shrug off the security guard.

Kristie, Lisa, Felicity, and Mario all stand and watch as he's escorted out of the bar, and once they finish their drinks, they head to Story nightclub down in South of Fifth.

As the night progresses, Kristie ends up getting really drunk, on very little alcohol. She's barely eaten over the past few weeks, so it's not surprising. The upside to being intoxicated is that she's numbed her pain, her heartache, to the point where she's dancing the night away.

She must admit, it feels good not to feel anything for a change; she's exhausted from living with such gut-wrenching agony every single day, it's draining her; to have a little break is doing her some good... for the first time in weeks, she finally has a break from feeling like she's going to die of a broken heart.

But sadly, when she comes home, all she wants is to fall into Enrique's arms; her heart is broken once again, as she knows that's not possible. She knows that they're better off apart, but it hurts like hell... it's torture.

As she gets undressed and has a quick shower, she finds herself crying as she stands under the powerful stream of water; why do things have to be this way. Being apart from Enrique might be the right thing to do, but why does it feel so wrong... so unnatural... so excruciatingly painful? Why can't things just go back to the way they were... back when they were so happy and nothing else mattered apart from the two of them... when all they ever focused on was each other... wanting to spend every waking moment together... not wanting to miss a thing... why can't things be like that again? All she wants is Enrique... he's all she's ever wanted... he's all she's ever needed.

She allows her tears to fall and fall, letting herself heave through her pain as her body releases some of her agony. She wants it to stop… but she knows she has to let it out, and she hopes she will feel better for it… even if it's a tiny bit better.

After a short while, she gathers herself and has a wash, then dries herself off before getting ready for bed. She then makes her way to the bedroom and gets into bed. With the alcohol already wearing off, her pain comes back ten-fold. The pain is too much to bear. She begins to cry uncontrollably, hugging Enrique's pillow as she sobs and sobs, crying herself to sleep once more.

Chapter 9
Monday, April 23rd, 2018
Enrique

Enrique has just found out that Kristie was out at the weekend; Sánchez has just called him and during their conversation, he mentioned that she was out in South Beach. Jealousy takes over Enrique's body and mind. He can't handle it. He's not jealous that she's gone out… he welcomes the fact that she's living her life… he's always encouraged her to do her own thing… what is bothering him is way beyond anything he can handle right now; what if she finds somebody else? He can't deal with the thought of another man touching the love of his life… his girl… his everything.

He twists his office chair so he can look out of the floor-to-ceiling window of his office, and gazes out across Downtown and the bay, toward her apartment building. What would he do if she found somebody else? How the fuck will he cope? Seeing her around Miami with another guy would be absolute torture for him. Yes, he knows they're apart... he knows he has no room to talk as *he* is the reason why they're not together anymore, but he can't stand to even consider the prospect of another man touching the lady he still so naturally considers as his. Kristie is part of him, she is his heart and soul... his world, his universe, and he loves her with his entire being, that will never change, and he has no idea how he's going to handle the day when she finds somebody else.

Kristie is the most beautiful lady in the world, and men will be falling at her feet, she won't be short of offers, and Enrique is well aware of this; when they would go out, men would constantly look at her, and he could never resist giving them the "she's mine," glare. He's not stupid, he knows that this will be a possibility, and it's almost certainly going to happen at some point, but he has no clue how he's going to deal with it... he *can't* deal with it.

He feels sick to the stomach, he wants to rush over to her spa and beg for her forgiveness, but like they've already said to each other many times, Enrique needs to change his ways, and this is something he can't seem to get a handle on either.

What the fuck is he going to do? He's sure as hell going to have to figure something out because this is unbearable.

He turns back to his computer and tries to busy himself with work, pushing down the raging jealousy as it boils inside of him.

* * *

Later that evening

As Enrique works well into the night, to his despair, he starts to have this strange shift of emotions once again, and the sense of relief is back, throwing him off course, just like every other time. He doesn't know how much more he can take, what with everything else he's feeling... the pain, the heartache... the raging jealousy... with this on top, he feels like he's about to explode!

One thing he does know is that he's not relieved due to anything relating to Kristie... it's something else... and that is what he's trying to figure out. He doesn't understand his feelings whatsoever; he never has when it comes to his darkness, but it would appear that since Kristie's left, he understands them even less. He has no idea what the hell is going on with him at all.

As he sits, looking out of the floor-to-ceiling window, he can see the view of the city lights, and to the right of the cityscape, he can see the bay, which is shrouded in darkness. He has to talk to Kristie... he has to hear her voice... he *needs* to hear her voice.

He finds his cell and makes the call.

"Hey, how's it going?" He says, as she answers.

"I'm good... busy day, ya know... just watching some TV." She replies, sounding exhausted. "How about you?"

"I'm good... been working all day... just finishing up."

"You at home or at work?"

"At home." He wants to tell her that he misses her... he wants her back... he's desperate for them to reconcile, but he holds back... he has to... but that doesn't stop him from wanting to, all the same.

"It's late, babe."

"I know... just had a lot to do today... some of it, I wanted to get a head start, ready for the morning...."

"I know... it's always good to be prepared...." She says, as she stands and walks toward the balcony. Once she's out on the terrace, she leans on the railing and looks out to the vast ocean, glistening in the moonlight. "I miss you." She whispers.

Enrique's heart breaks into a billion pieces. He stays quiet. He can't speak.

"I'm sorry." She whispers.

"No... no, it's OK." He says back sweetly. "I feel the very same."

"Then, what are we doing?" Kristie asks. She can feel herself getting upset, but she tries to stay strong.

"I know," Enrique says with sadness.

"Why are we apart... why can't we be together? Why are you there, and I'm here, Enrique... why?"

"Because of me." He says, looking down with shame... he's ashamed... ashamed of himself for not being able to remedy this situation.

"Oh, Enrique... I love you so much... please...."

"I know, baby... I love you so much, too... more than anything in the world... I'm trying, I really am... but I can't... it just...."

"But, why... why?" Kristie's voice is beginning to break... she reigns herself in, trying to hold back the tears. She knows and understands why things are the way they are, but her emotions are getting the better of her.

"Krissy, please… you know why." He pleads.

"But, you miss me… I miss you… we love each other, surely, we can find a way… surely, it's that simple… we both want the same things."

"We do… I want to be with you more than anything… I would do anything to be with you right now… to have you in my arms… to spend the rest of my life with you… to marry you… everything… that's all I want, babe… you know that."

"Then, why can't we do all those things… why can't we fix this, Enrique… if we both really want this… we can find a way… we can make the changes we need to make…."

"It's not that simple, babe… you know that."

"It is, though… we're two people with so much drive and focus… if we want something in life, we go after it… we work our asses off to get it… why can't the same be done with our relationship?" She's beginning to get agitated now; her heartache is turning to frustration.

"So, you think I'm not working at this? You think that I'm just sitting here, letting this shit happen, because I want it to?"

"I didn't say that." She snaps back.

"Well, it sure as hell sounds like it from where I'm standing!"

"Enrique."

"No, Kristie... you know what I go through... you know I'm trying... doing my best... and I'm sorry that my best isn't good enough!" Before he can say anymore, he hangs up the phone; he has to get out of this situation as quickly as he can... and he knows it's because he can't stand to be challenged when it comes to dealing with his shit.

He puts his cell down firmly on the glass desk, and walks out of the office, then into the kitchen. He makes some cafécito.

As he waits for the coffee to brew, he can feel his heart racing. All he can hear is Kristie telling him that coffee isn't a good idea when you feel anxious... from who the hell knows where, he manages a smile, as he recalls the countless times she's told him this... to which he would reply, "I've been drinking it since before I was born," and ain't that the truth! Cubans love their coffee, and Enrique is most definitely not the exception when it comes to that statement!

As he pours the coffee into the white espresso cup, which is sitting on the sparkling black quartz counter in front of him, he thinks about his conversation with Kristie. He knows he was in the wrong, once again, but he does feel a little judged when it comes to his way of dealing with things. He really does feel he's doing his best, but he also knows it's not good enough. Both he and Kristie are brokenhearted over this, and the ball is technically in his court, but he genuinely can't face it... it's like every time he tries to do something about it, he reaches a dead end or a roadblock; he has no idea what to do. But one thing he does know is he has to call her back and apologize. He shouldn't have hung up on her that way; she's upset and is struggling with her own feelings with all this... at the end of the day, she's the innocent party in all of this. All she did was fall in love with him and give him everything... he's the one that fucked it all up.

He heads back to the office and calls her back. She doesn't answer. He calls again. Still no answer. He tries again. She finally answers.

"Hey." He says, in a downcast tone.

"Enrique, I don't think it's a good idea for us to be in contact at the moment." She says firmly. She's pissed off, and she's doing absolutely nothing to hide it. "It's obvious that it's not the right thing to do right now... and if I'm honest, I think I was naïve to think that we could be friends so soon after everything." She continues. "Maybe it's something we can revisit in the future... but for now, I don't think we should be in contact."

"Krissy, please... don't do this." He pleads. "I'm sorry... I'm so sorry for lashing out the way I do... I'm sorry that I'm the reason we're not together... I'm sorry that I'm the reason for your heartache and pain... I'm sorry for everything... I really am... but you have to see that I'm doing my very best... it's not good enough, I know... but I am."

"You might well be, Enrique... but I can't keep going through this same old cycle, over and over again... it's not doing either of us any good... and the way you speak to me sometimes is disgusting... I'm not having it, Enrique... it's not on."

"I know... I swear I'll do better... I don't know what's happening to me... I feel like I'm swinging in so many different directions right now... I don't know what the hell is going on with me... please... please rethink this... please don't do this."

Kristie goes quiet as she thinks about how she feels about this. The truth is, she doesn't know. She likes speaking to him on the phone, and she still can't imagine him not being in her life, but at the same time, she doesn't need his disrespect... his mood swings, and rants. She knows what he's going through, but at the same time, she knows that this is the reason why she left.

"Please, baby... please forgive me... I'm so, so sorry... I really am...." He pleads.

"Look, Enrique, I understand what you're going through, but you can't keep doing this... you can't keep lashing out at me and hanging up, just because I say something you don't want to hear."

"I know." He agrees.

"I know how impulsive you are... I know how passionate and fiery you get... I mean, that's part of the reason why I love you so much... but the downside to that is too much for me... the downside to how fiery you are... your stubbornness, is another level, especially right now... and when all I'm doing is trying to help you... when I know you're drinking too much... or whatever... everything I do is out of love... even now."

"I know, baby, I know... and I love you for that... I just struggle, sometimes... struggle to accept help."

"I know you do... but, Enrique, you have to find a way... this is no life... and we want to be together... we both do... that much is obvious." She sighs. "So much time is being wasted... you get one life... and I don't want to spend it this way... and I sure as hell know you don't, either... so please, babe... please... deal with this."

"I will… I promise I will… I will figure it out." He says with deep meaning.

As he puts the phone down to Kristie, he knows he argued with her because he can't handle his emotions, and even worse, he can't handle the thought of her being with someone else, although he will never tell her that. He's been putting himself under so much pressure over recent months, as he knows he has to get his shit together, but still hasn't found a way; he has to have faith that he will… he has to… he wants Kristie back in his life for good, and knows that this is the only way. But for now, he's going to get his head down and work until he crashes, whenever that might be.

* * *

Somewhere during the early hours, laying alone in his super king-sized bed, Enrique is dreaming about a time when he and Kristie made love out in the blazing Caribbean sunshine in the middle of the tropical waters on one of the boats, and then at the Bahamas property. As he floats in a sea of blissful, loving memories, he then drifts to another time when he was driving them up to a charity gala in Lauderdale, and they were listening to his 80s rock playlist in the blue Range Rover SVR.

After he sang various songs to her, like "Give Me All Your Love" and "Still of the Night" by Whitesnake, "Paradise City" by Guns N' Roses,

"Bad Medicine" and "Livin' On A Prayer" by Bon Jovi, plus one of their favorites, "Born to Be My Baby" also, by Bon Jovi, all in his usual rock star fashion, pretending to play the drums on the steering wheel, as he danced in his seat; he then sang the lyrics to "Naughty Naughty" by John Parr. He literally followed the words to the song and glided his hand up her leg, feeling the silk of her stocking, before going even further than the song suggests and pushed his fingers past the top of her stocking, to her panties....

Before they even made it to Fort Lauderdale, they ended up making love wildly, somewhere off the I-95, away from prying eyes! Kristie's nails were in his back once again, drawing blood, staining his shirt; he was loving every minute of it! They made it to the gala just in time, and Enrique was thankful for his black Armani Tuxedo jacket concealing his blood-stained shirt... it was hot as fuck... it was their beautiful, yet naughty little secret, just like so many times before.

The following Saturday, during a boy's boat day, Sánchez, and García teased him about the scratches on his back; his back was covered in scars. He tried to downplay it, saying that it was from a palm in the garden in Manatee, but they didn't buy it... it was pretty obvious what the scratches were from, but he would never admit that to them!

That evening, when he got home, he was looking all tanned and muscly... the second he saw Kristie, she rushed to him, then jumped up to him, and they made love passionately... so passionately, she added more scratches to his already tender back; he loved every minute of it once again.

Then, suddenly, he wakes up abruptly and realizes this is not his reality... once again, it was all a dream... what a tragic state he's living in.

He rolls on his back, placing the back of his forearm over his eyes, begging to fall back into his dream... his reality is too devastating... too brutal... it's torture to endure. His mind then drifts to a similar past moment when they were driving down The Keys... something Enrique always used to avoid before he met Kristie. One of the boats or his helicopter was always a better option, due to the slow-moving traffic and amount of single-lane highways... but when he met Kristie, that all changed, because she used to love the drive down there, as it was so pretty... and he could never deny that.

As he lies there, he realizes he must have been triggered by dreaming of him singing Bon Jovi to Kristie in such a dramatic way, just as he always used to, especially when he was fooling around on the stage at a karaoke bar! He now has a perfect vision of them driving down The Keys in his blue Ferrari with the top down, singing to Bon Jovi, and the song he's remembering right now is "I'll Be There for You."

They're singing the lyrics at the top of their lungs, dancing in their seats, and rocking their heads back and forth, having the time of their lives. With his eyes still closed, he shakes his head with sadness and disbelief. Who'd have thought that something so carefree and fun, could now be turned into something so painful, so agonizing, and there's even a soundtrack to his feelings, to boot.

Every lyric to that song resonates with him and cuts through him like shards of glass, shredding his entire being to smithereens. Even the part about her Birthday is hitting him hard... it's Kristie's Birthday next week, and he's dreading it. At the time, neither of them would believe it was even possible for them to be in this situation only months later. How did this happen? One minute, you're so happy, without a care in the world, and the next, you have the rug pulled from under you.

It is now 4am... and after laying with his eyes closed, wondering how the fuck any of this ever happened, he feels frustrated and heartbroken all at once... he knows how they got here... they got here because of him and his shit!

There's nothing else he can do but work out like crazy until he collapses, then get showered and head to work until dark.

Chapter 10
Tuesday, April 24th, 2018

This evening, Enrique is at his grandparent's restaurant. As sounds of salsa ring in the air, he's sitting out on the terrace with his father, José, and his grandfather, Pablo. They're drinking cafécito and smoking some Cuban cigars as they talk about their days, and a little bit about Leon and the amazing work he's doing at the center, plus Enrique's plans for Manatee Bay. It's nice to sit with his father and grandfather, shooting the breeze in the carefree manner they always do these days, as there have been times when Enrique could feel a little tension between them. Enrique has always put it down to a past conflict when his mom died, but thankfully, everything is good now, and Enrique is more than happy about it.

As they talk in Spanish amongst themselves, the ballad version of "Tu Amor Me Hace Bien" by Marc Anthony begins to play over the sound system in the restaurant. As *their* song plays, suddenly Enrique's mind fills with thoughts of Kristie; her curvaceous figure as she elegantly sways to the music, as she dances with him... the sensation of having her so close to him, as they move in perfect sync with each other. Her smile... her scent... her glorious dark brown eyes as they gaze into his, with a love so pure and unconditional, he falls in love with her all over again. Whatever happened? How could it all go so wrong? How could this have gotten so out of control that they're no longer together and haven't seen each other in weeks? There was a time when the thought of being apart for even one night was unbearable, but three weeks without as much as a kiss? It's torture... it's hell on earth... if only he could find a way.

"Enrique... papi... are you OK?" José asks, full of deep concern.

Enrique doesn't answer.

"Papi... Enrique." José says a little louder.

"Sorry... what?" Enrique says, sounding a little dazed and out of it.

"We lost you for a bit," José says. "Papi... what's going on?"

"Uhhh... just a little preoccupied, that's all... ya know," Enrique explains, trying to sound casual and like it's nothing, but his eyes give him away.

"Papi... please... talk to her... talk to her properly." José pleads. "You have to do this... for her... for yourself... it's been going on for too long now... please, papi."

"I can't, dad," Enrique replies, shaking his head with devastation. "I just can't."

"You can... you can do anything you set your mind to... you can design and build the most incredible buildings... you organize all your charity work and help so many people... you have achieved so much... you've made the impossible possible more times than I can count... don't let fear get in the way of the best thing that's ever happened to you... the love of your life... life's too short... come on, papi... find a way... just like you have with so many other things in life." José says.

"I would if I could... trust me." Enrique shakes his head once more. "I don't know... I don't know... I mean, even if I did find a way... is it too late now? Have things gone too far... have *I* gone too far." He shakes his head again, before puffing on his cigar and exhaling the smooth smoke; today, it's like he's lost any positivity toward his situation with Kristie... he's desperately struggling to see a way out of this right now. He wants her back more than anything, but has he destroyed things to the point of no return? He hopes not, but it's a serious concern of his due to his very own stupidity and actions. "I behaved so disgustingly... Krissy didn't deserve any of it... I wonder if she will even be able to forgive me... even if she wants to... when it comes down to it... will she be able to?"

"Of course, she will... and papito... it's never too late." Pablo says, with reassurance, straightening his fedora as he takes another puff of his cigar. "It's never too late... especially for you and Kristie. You're meant to be... everybody knows that... the way you look at each other... the way you are together... it's so obvious to us all that you two were put on this earth to be together."

"Thank you, Abuelo... and I agree with you... we were meant to be together... and I will never love like that again... in fact, I never *will* love again... but I wonder if too much time has passed... so much happened... and I can't seem to get a grip... it's not fair on her... she deserves peace."

"You both do, papá," José adds. "You both love each other so much... and I know you will find a way... the two of you will find a way back to each other... I just know it."

"Me too," Pablo says. "Me too... just give it time, papito... just give it time... it's been a lot for you... you've been through so much... give yourself time... and it will come... trust me."

"Thank you, Abuelo... thank you," Enrique replies sweetly, looking at his grandfather with tear-filled eyes.

Suddenly, he can feel hope flicker in his heart. Aside from Kristie, this is probably the most honest he's ever been about his feelings relating to his situation with her; could this be the start of things to come? Is this what those feelings of relief were about? Have the tears he shed when Kristie left, cleared something inside of him? Could this be him finally beginning to open up? He hopes so. He's never really had a conversation with his grandfather like this before. Yes, he's talked like this with his father, but he's actually feeling a little more comfortable discussing things with his grandfather now, too. In his mind, he prays that he will figure it out and finally open up to Kristie completely and be honest with her about what's going on inside of him... and that day can't come soon enough!

* * *

Thursday, April 26th, 2018

Enrique works and works, ignoring his feelings, acting like everything is OK; his emotions are only getting more and more complicated and beyond impossible to understand... this is something he can't get his head around; it's almost like the more he's trying to get a handle on things, the more complex his feelings are getting. How is this so?

On a positive note, he has taken on board what his father and grandfather have advised him to do, but he still can't seem to execute it, although he has taken the little victory that something must be changing inside of him, as he was a little more open to his grandfather than he has ever been; he hopes that this is the start of something good!

He and Kristie have spoken on the phone every day, and things have been calm between them. They have kept their conversations about general day-to-day topics, and nothing else, which is best for both of them.

Enrique's dreams of him and Kristie are getting more and more frequent. When he does manage to get some sleep, all he seems to do is dream about Kristie. These dreams are generally about past experiences together, and they are all just that: dreamy. He wakes feeling like they are real life and then gets hit with the harsh reality that they are nothing but a figment of his imagination... it's torture.

He has to admit, when he wakes to find this out, all he wants to do is go back to sleep again so he can keep dreaming about the love of his life, but that's not possible, as he never can get back to sleep. Enrique Cruz has excelled at many things in his life, but sleep isn't one of them, and right now, his insomnia is worse than it's ever been. Not only does he have his darkness to deal with, he now has to try to navigate his way through the hell that is his life without Kristie, and he's not doing a very good job of it.

Even when he goes out with Sánchez and García to try to have a break from it all, he hears songs that remind him of him and Kristie; everywhere he goes, are constant reminders of her, it's almost like life didn't exist before her... and music was such a huge part of their lives... music always seems to follow him in life, be it in a positive or negative way.

As he sits in the VIP area of one of Miami's world-renowned clubs, he hears "Back Together" by Hardsoul Featuring Ron Carroll... every single lyric hits him harder than the last; this song explains everything. Before he can stop himself, he reaches to the inside pocket of his jacket for his cell; he has to text Kristie.

I miss you.
I can't live without you.
xxxxx

His thumb hovers over the send button for a few moments, then thoughts of all the hurt and pain he's caused her... all the nights he left her alone... the mean things he said to her... the heartache he subjected her to... the drinking... the broken promises... the picking of fights... the anger... the mood swings and outbursts... he can't put her through anymore... he can't do that to her again... he loves her too much... he loves her more than anything in the world... and that love is what is stopping him from sending this text.

He deletes the message, slips his cell back into his jacket pocket, finds the bottle of vodka on the table, and pours himself another shot, then knocks it back before pouring another, in a desperate bid to numb his self-inflicted agony.

Chapter 11
Friday, April 27th, 2018

Enrique wakes at 7am following a late night and gets himself ready for another day at the office, then late afternoon, he will head to a construction site to check on the progress. In the gym, with his 80s playlist blasting, he powers through set after set of lifting a ton of over bearing weights; his mind may be fucked, but his body is going to be perfectly tuned.

As he lifts the last rep of this set, "Always on My Mind" by Pet Shop Boys comes on over the sound system; as the lyrics resonate with him, he nearly drops the heavy chest press on himself.

"FUCK!" He curses out loud at himself. He forces his mind back to the job at hand and manages to place the weight back on its rack, before sitting up on the bench and wiping his face with a towel.

As the song plays, he feels winded and heartbroken. This is fucking shit... constant reminders of his fuck ups... his failures... what he did to Kristie... to their relationship... to his life! Will it ever stop? Will he ever catch a break? This song literally describes the last few months of their relationship, and he feels like absolute shit about it... he was such an asshole to her, and he still is. She was the best thing that ever happened to him, and he just let her walk out of his life... and for what? A life alone, suffering... in more pain than he's ever been in... while Kristie is heartbroken, living without him across the bay in her apartment... something has to give at some point... it has to.

He turns the music off through fear of any more reminders... he's had his fill of the painful memories he keeps being forced to relive; he loves his music, but he can't deal with it right now. As he finishes off his workout in silence, his eyes glance up at one of the TVs on the wall, and he notices a cartel called Los Fantasmas has been named once again for the murder of members of another organization that works out of Miami; a triple homicide, this time. They're one of the most feared cartels in the world, and not a single agency can catch up with them, it's like a sick game of cat and mouse... hence their name... The Ghosts.

As Enrique finishes another set of stomach crunches, he sits up and watches the news report spread across the screen in subtitles. "Fucking assholes," he mutters as he watches the muted TV. He might have an interest in the underworld and read books or watch movies, but he hates drugs; he was brought up that way. His father was so strict with this when he was growing up. He gave him the "You take drugs, and you will die" type lecture, and to be fair, this worked for the most part, aside from a little dabble in his late teens. He tried cocaine once and wondered what all the fuss was about. He and his friends, Sánchez and García, wondered if it was something to do with the extreme amounts of cafécito they had subjected their bodies to over the years, who knows, but it was most definitely a non-event for them.

He stands, turns off the TV with the remote and picks up his empty espresso cup before heading downstairs to take a shower and get dressed, ready for work. He might have a shave today and make a little more effort than he has been recently. This is unheard of as Enrique is always clean-shaven, especially since he's been with Kristie, she's not a fan of stubble as it hurts her face when they kiss. Not that he has to think about this now, unfortunately, but he feels better about himself when he's clean-shaven, plus he's trying to do better and take better care of himself. He's been running on coffee and alcohol for the past few weeks, and it just won't do. He's usually a clean eater for a majority of the time and limits alcohol, but recently, he's not been taking care of himself. He can't get sick, he doesn't *get* sick, so he'd better start to look after himself!

He heads downstairs, and Gabriela, his housekeeper, is making him breakfast; spinach and tomato omelet with wholewheat toast. He walks into the kitchen and greets her, checking in on her and the kids. Before heading to work.

As Emilio drives him to work in the white Maybach, he thinks about the fact that it's Kristie's birthday on Wednesday and wonders what she will be doing. Every year, by now, he would have found her the perfect gift, or gifts, and his plans for her big day would be well underway. This year will be the first year that they haven't spent her birthday together since they met, and the first year he has not celebrated the anniversary of the day he first laid eyes on her: May 3rd, a date that will go down in his very own history book as the day his life changed forever.

When he first saw Kristie, his whole world turned upside down; he fell in love... hard. He didn't know what on earth was happening to him, and he had no choice but to go with it as it was a force more powerful than he was, and it still is. He still classes that day as the best day of his life... and he's said many times that it's the day his life began, and he still feels very much that way.

As devastated as he is that he and Kristie have parted ways, he still feels as lucky as he did then, to have met her and to have had somebody as incredible as her to share such a beautiful time in his life... his only regret is that he couldn't quite make it... he doesn't have what it takes, to give her what she deserves, although all his friends and now his family, as he has now told them, have all said that they will be back together... just give it time.

As Emilio pulls the Maybach into the parking garage of his company building, he wonders if there might be some truth in this... maybe he will finally find the courage to face his demons once and for all… he hopes he will… and he hopes that day will come sooner rather than later!

* * *

Later that evening

Enrique's had a shit day at work, and to make matters worse, he's done nothing but beat himself up inside about the fact that he can't get his shit together and fix things with Kristie. It's like the answer is right there in front of him, and every time he tries to grab hold of it… it slips through his fingers.

To top it all, he can't seem to control his feelings of jealousy as he thinks about the possibility of somebody else dating her. He knows that Kristie isn't the kind of girl to go out on the town to find a man, and he's pretty sure that she's not interested in that right now anyway, but she is so beautiful, and he knows that this is going to happen at some point.

He loves and misses her so damn much, and he hates himself for what he has done. He's fucked up a treat, and he has no way of fixing it, as the only way of fixing it is so impossible to him… he's so angry and frustrated he wants to scream! On top of that, it's Kristie's Birthday on Wednesday, and he's not going to share it with her, which he also feels like complete shit about; he's such a mess… an angry, heartbroken, desperate, fucked-up mess, and a coward at that! And on top of all of that... he's had a day from hell, where everything has gone wrong... he's really not in the mood for anything other than a few hours in the gym, then perhaps going out with the boys to escape his shit for a while; he will see how he feels after some exercise... perhaps he will give himself a night off tonight, as he had a pretty heavy night last night.

As he makes his way upstairs to get changed, his cell rings; it's Kristie.

"Hey." He answers, trying to sound like everything's OK, when that couldn't be further from the truth.

"Hey... how's things? How was your night?" She asks. They haven't spoken much today, and they didn't speak at all last night. Earlier on, while she was getting coffee, she overheard somebody talking about Enrique being wasted in a club last night; she hates that people are talking about him this way... and she knows he will hate it too.

"I'm fine... all is OK... last night was good." He replies, sounding a little suspicious of her tone; she sounds like she's fishing or knows something, but he tries to ignore it. "How are you?" He asks.

"Are you really OK, though, babe? I'm worried about you." She says quietly, getting straight to the point.

And there it is!

"There's no need." He snaps in Spanish; his tone is glacial. "And like I've said before, why *are* you worried?" He's curt and to the point.

"Oh, come on, Enrique." She replies in Spanish. "You know why I'm worried... just because I left...."

"Exactly... *you* left... so what I get up to in my free time... or, even what I get up to in my not-so-free time, has nothing to do with you... it's no concern of yours... so quit keep asking me if I'm *really* OK!" He's pissed off and is doing absolutely nothing to hide it; he's had it! "Whatever your little chismosos are reporting back to you is highly inaccurate... so please... do yourself a favor and stop listening to their shit!" He hangs up the phone and promptly calls the boys. "Wanna go out... I can get us a table...."

"We already have one, Lover Boy!" Sánchez says. "At Liquid Gold... you up for some sexy women and some extremely over-priced liquor?!"

"Not so much the women... but the liquor... yes... I need to party... fuck this shit!" Enrique says.

"Oh, come on, Pretty Boy... the best way to get over somebody is to get under somebody else!" García jests.

"No way!" Enrique says firmly, he can't even imagine touching another woman, even with the way things are with him and Kristie right now, he knows she's the only lady for him, and in his mind, he knows he will never be with another, ever again... he's done... if he can't have Kristie... he doesn't want anybody.

"You're no fun... perhaps if you get laid, you'll cheer the fuck up!"

"I'm cheered up plenty," Enrique says, all matter-of-fact and straight to the point. "Now, you both coming here first or shall I meet you at one of your houses of debauchery?"

"We'll meet you at yours," Sánchez confirms.

"OK, cool."

"Get your glad rags on... cause we're gonna par-tay!" García hollers, before they say their goodbyes.

As he puts his phone down to his friends, he notices a text from Kristie.

*I don't think it's
a good idea to keep
in contact.
It's not good for
either of us.
I love and care*

about you, but I can't
have you in my life,
right now.
Please, take care
of yourself.
K
xx

As he reads the message, he can't agree more with her, as he can't see past the red mist of anger that's clouding his judgment. Why the hell would he want this shit in his life anyway? He texts her back.

OK.

Then, without a second thought, he places his cell down on the nightstand and makes his way to the closet to get changed, then heads up to the gym for another workout before getting ready to go out with the boys. He's angry. There's no way anybody is telling him what to do with his life... at the end of the day, Kristie left him... she didn't want to be with him anymore... so why does she keep nagging at him about his shit... it has nothing to do with her anymore.

Then, out of nowhere, a tiny voice is whispering in his head. "You're being unreasonable, Enrique... she only cares, and she certainly wasn't telling you what to do with your life, she was merely checking that you're OK.

He ignores it. He's done… why's he talking to her anyway… it's over… she's gone… left… he has to get on with his life and live it the way he sees fit; he doesn't need anybody telling him what to do, he's a free man, and he wants to go out tonight and have a good time… and that's exactly what he will do… with nobody to answer to, but himself!

* * *

Kristie

Enrique's response speaks volumes. She's done the right thing. She's had it with him and his mood swings and outbursts. She was only trying to help and be there for him; it's obvious there's some truth in what she's heard due to his reaction, and the fact that she's called him a few times and he's still been in bed at lunchtime; this is so unlike him, he's always up super early on weekends, as well as weekdays, it's blatant that he's not coming home until at least breakfast time, for him to sleep in this late… even when he used to go out until the early hours, he'd still be up and ready for work by 7am.

The trouble is, although she knows she's done the right thing, it still hurts like hell, but she has to try to rise above it; she doesn't need this shit in her life. At the end of the day, she left Enrique for a reason, and this is that very reason. She knows he doesn't like things like this being pointed out, and he sure as hell doesn't like to be told what to do… although that wasn't what she was trying to do…

she's never told him what to do, ever... she's just extremely worried about him. With all said and done, she still loves him just as much as she did when they were together, and she would hate for anything to happen to him.

As she sits down on the sofa, she knows what he will be doing right now... she doesn't need anybody to tell her... but what can she do? She considers contacting José, but she's worried that Enrique will feel betrayed by her if she does, also it could make things worse. He's so private about things, and when she was still living with him, she mentioned speaking to José about things, and Enrique refused to. He said that his father knew very little about the situation, and he wanted it to stay that way.

She sits alone in her beautiful beachfront apartment, with nothing but her conflicted thoughts and emotions to keep her company. She loves that man so damn much, but he's so impossible for her to be around. She knows he's behaving the way he is because he's angry at himself... deep down, she knows this... she knows he's blaming himself for everything and hates that he can't open up to her... but that's still no excuse to make her life hell in the process. Why do things have to be so complicated? Why can't he just talk about what's going on with him? Why can't she be enough to help him get through this pain and heartache? Why can't they be together? She misses him so much, yet she's so angry with him, for speaking to her that way. How can somebody so sweet and gentlemanly, become so rude and dismissive... dismissive of her concerns... dismissive of *her*?

Kristie is beyond heartbroken over the situation, but she knows she has to stay strong... she has to push through this pain... she has to figure out a way to deal with all of this, as things sure as hell don't seem to be looking up, in any way... if anything, they're only getting worse. Has she been a fool all along, to think that she and Enrique could still be friends? Has she been naïve to believe that she could perhaps have him in her life in some way? Right now, she's feeling like she really is a fool... a fool that only ever sees the good in people... well, perhaps it's time for things to change. She doesn't need to be spoken to that way... to be treated the way Enrique has been treating her recently... so yes, maybe it is time for things to change... maybe she should leave Enrique to his own devices and focus on herself... maybe she should really think of herself... perhaps the time has come for Kristie to put herself first... and let Enrique worry about his own life?

As her thoughts float through her mind, she knows in her heart that she could never let go of him... he's the love of her life... her world... her everything... *still*... even after everything... but sadly, things don't always work out the way we plan them, and you have to find a way to live with the life, the universe has mapped out for you... but

right now, she knows that that is too hard to face...
right now, everything is hard... so difficult... even
getting out of bed in the morning is so difficult, but
she has to keep going... no matter how hard things
get, she will never give up... as they say, when
you're in hell, you've gotta keep walking... and she
will keep on walking... she has to believe that
things will get better... she has to... there's no
other way.

* * *

Enrique

As his night goes on, the alcohol is flowing nicely,
and Enrique is finally loosening up. He knows he
overreacted to Kristie earlier, and he also knows
that the truth hurts... she was telling him how it is,
and he didn't like it... so, as per usual, he ranted at
her about how she didn't know what she was
talking about, then cut her off. As he thinks about
his actions, he might still be mad at her, but he
feels like shit about the way he behaved... he needs
to apologize to her tomorrow. He knows she said
what she said in her text, but he feels he has to
apologize to her if she will allow him, and then he
will respect her decision if that's what she wants,
as much as he knows that is the last thing he
wants... all he wants is her... that's all he's ever
wanted... but he's too much of a fuck up, to make it
happen.

Looking hot as hell, wearing a custom-made black suit and blue shirt, Enrique's sitting in the VIP area of one of Miami's super clubs with the boys, minding his own business, taking in the scene as he sits with García. The vibe is on point, the DJ is spinning the perfect beats, and the atmosphere is electric, but it's totally lost on Enrique, as his heart and mind are not in it... as always, all he can think about is Kristie.

Then, suddenly, out of nowhere, he overhears somebody talking about a guy named Peter. His ears prick up as Kristie's ex-boyfriend is called Peter, and he's at the very top of Enrique's shitlist; he's a fucking asshole, and Enrique would love nothing more than to wipe him off the face of the planet, but he keeps telling himself that he has to be the better person.

He tries to ignore the conversation, but the men are being so loud that it's completely impossible to ignore... then to his disgust, he hears them mention Peter and Kristie in the same sentence. That's it... he's listening hard, and he's not going to miss a single detail.

Kristie hasn't mentioned anything about seeing Peter, but that doesn't mean it hasn't happened, as she knows exactly how he feels about him. Enrique finds this hard to admit, even to himself, but he's living in a permanent state of anger, and that anger is simmering, ready to boil over at the slightest provocation, and as difficult as it is for him to accept, he knows that Kristie is well aware of this… so it would be plausible that she simply hasn't told him about Peter, to save him from himself.

As he listens on, it would appear that Peter was trying to get back with Kristie during the weekend she went out, as he'd heard that she had split from Enrique… this sends Enrique into overdrive… he's gonna kill the fucker!

He turns to look at the men and then glances around the club with wide eyes smoldering with fury, hyped up on adrenaline and hatred toward this sorry excuse for a human being; Peter is nowhere to be seen.

García sees and hears everything. He gives Enrique a look so serious it stops him in his tracks, although he's raging inside right now. "No!" García says, reading his friend perfectly.

"I'm gonna find that fucking cunt, and fucking kill him!" Enrique seethes in Spanish; his handsome face is dark and menacing.

"No… Enrique… no, you're not." García repeats, keeping the conversation going in Spanish.

"Yes, I fucking am." He stands, getting ready to leave.

García stands and pushes him back down on the white leather couch in the VIP area of the club. Enrique shrugs him off of him. "Get the fuck off of me." He snaps, getting ready to get back up again.

"No," García repeats. "You're not going anywhere… he's not worth it… now, stay and have another drink."

"No… I don't want another drink… I want to find that fucking asshole, Peter, and fucking kill him." Enrique fumes. "How fucking dare he even approach Kristie after everything he's done to her… fucking cunt… I've told him to stay the fuck away from her!" He's seeing red, and there's no way back for him.

Sánchez walks over to the two men, laughing as he puts a girl's number in the inside pocket of his YSL suit jacket. "Another conquest for later." He says, full of cheer, and then he sees his friend's faces and loses his good vibe instantly. "What the fuck is it?" He asks, as he sits down in front of them. "Qué pasó?"

García tells him, in short, about what's happened.

"If he's as much as laid a finger on her… I fucking swear to God…." Enrique seethes. "He thinks that because of what's happened… between me and Krissy, he can get away with his shit… well, he needs to be stopped." He fumes. His face darkens even more, and his tone becomes what can only be described as venomous. "If he's as much as laid a finger on her... I fucking swear to God...."

"He wouldn't have... because Kristie wouldn't have let it happen," Sánchez says.

"Exactly." García agrees.

"Krissy would have dealt with it herself... there's no need for you to get involved," Sánchez says, trying to defuse Enrique's fury, just like his friend García. "Leave it alone." He says simply, waving his hand at Enrique like it's nothing; he's trying to pacify the situation, as he knows exactly where this could lead. Enrique's so ramped up right now that anything is possible, and he has to protect his friend from doing something he regrets.

"I want to kill that asshole." Enrique snipes, trying to get back up again, but both his friends stop him; he may be six feet four, of solid muscle, but Sánchez and García work out too, and they can more than handle him together.

"Well, you're not going to," Sánchez says, pouring him another shot of vodka. He hands it to him. "Now, drink this... and move on."

Enrique's eyes glare into Sánchez's for a few moments, and then he takes the shot glass from him and knocks it back, wiping his mouth as he places the glass down on the table firmly in front of him.

"Right… good," García says, patting Enrique on the back. "Now… let's forget about this shit… and enjoy our night… just like we came here to do."

"I told him to stay the fuck away from her… I fucking warned him… he knows what will happen if he even approaches her!" Enrique rants. "If he's even touched her… I swear to God." He says with an evil face, shaking his head at the same time.

"He hasn't touched her, papo," Sánchez says with certainty. "Kristie wouldn't let him near her… he repulses her… you know that… she would have handled it… it's all been dealt with… and it's nothing for you to worry about."

"Yeah, bro… relax… Krissy's a good girl… she can handle herself… it's all good." García confirms.

They finally calm Enrique down and end up having a good night. Surprisingly, Enrique is home at a fairly reasonable hour… mainly because he knows that he desperately wants to speak to Kristie before she goes to work. He has to check that she's OK, and he has to apologize to her as a matter of priority.

Chapter 12
Saturday, April 28th, 2018

Enrique gets up early to call Kristie and apologize to her before she goes to work. He has to clear the air with her, and he really doesn't want her having this on her mind while she's trying to serve her clients; he also has to ask her about Peter.

"I'm sorry for calling you... I know you said what you said in your text... but... I...."

"It's OK," Kristie says quietly. She's actually glad she's heard from him. As much as she knows it's sensible for them to take a break from communicating with each other, she feels good that he's called her... just like always... everything is so confusing.

"I... I don't want to disrespect your wishes... I... I just couldn't leave things the way they were... I just feel a strong need to apologize to you for flying off the handle the way I did... I'm so sorry... the way I acted... my behavior... was totally uncalled for, not to mention disgusting and disrespectful...."

"It's OK... I just... Enrique... you can't keep talking to me that way... I don't need it."

"I know... and I am so, so sorry... please forgive me... I can't apologize enough... I was disgraceful to you... all you were doing was checking that I was OK... you were worried about me... and I love you for that, I really do."

"I was... that's all I do... worry about you... when I'm asking you things like that... it's always out of worry and concern... nothing else."

"I know... and I'm so sorry... please remember that it's me that I'm angry at... not you... please... it's never you... it's always me... this is my problem, not yours... and I'm so sorry for making it your problem... for keep making it your problem... I'm just so frustrated... all the time... frustrated that I can't mend things... do what needs to be done... and I lash out... just like always... I just get so impulsive about things... act first... think later...."

"I know... I know you do, Enrique... that's you... it's always you." She manages a small smile, although she's still mad at him.

"Always." He says, managing a smile, too. "And I'm trying to work on that."

"Yeah... well, not sure if that will ever change." Her voice sounds a little more upbeat as she means what she says.

"Hmmm, well, I'll never stop trying... I'll die trying... I mean, us Cubans... have a bit of a rep for it."

"I should say." She smiles.

"Yes... well, I'm trying to retrain myself... rewire my brain... but it would appear that it's a hard nut to crack."

"I can only imagine." She smiles. In fairness, this is a characteristic she actually quite likes about Enrique, but like everything, there's a bad side to it.

Their conversation goes on for a short while, and they talk about random things, and then he asks her if she saw Peter. She says that she did see him, and he did ask her back, but she refused and told him to leave her alone, which he did.

"Why didn't you tell me?" He asks urgently. "Did he hurt you in any way? What the hell happened?"

"Enrique, I didn't say anything because I know how you feel about him... and no... he didn't do anything... it was dealt with quickly... I sorted it." She says. "I don't need you fighting my battles... I can take care of myself... just like I have been doing, long since before I met you."

"OK, OK... I just... I can deal with him." He's almost begging for her to give him the permission to do this... she just has to say the word. "He could never be an issue again."

"No... no, you won't... just leave it alone... please," Kristie says firmly. "Christ, Enrique, what were we just talking about? Seriously... stop!" She lets out a slow breath. "You can't control everything... and go around "dealing" with people... it's crazy to even think that."

"Hmm, well, OK... but only because I would do anything for you."

"Enrique... I mean it... I never want to speak about that man again... he makes my skin crawl... please."

"OK... I promise." He says, feeling disappointed that he won't get the chance to teach the little prick one final lesson; Enrique isn't a violent man, but this guy has a way of pushing his buttons, making jail time seem like a small price to pay for the sheer satisfaction he would get from beating the living shit out of the sorry excuse for a man!

Once they end their call, Enrique feels good, although frustrated about the Peter situation, but at least he and Kristie are on good terms again; he has to stop this back and forth with her... he has to control his temper.

Starting the way he means to go on, he heads up to the gym and murders a three-hour workout filled with intense cardio, set after set of over-bearing weights, plus hundreds and hundreds of various stomach crunches... he will clear his mind if it kills him!

Chapter 13
Sunday, April 29th, 2018

Leon walks through the foyer of the penthouse and into the great room, glancing around to see where Enrique is.

"Hey, bro!" Enrique says, sounding way more cheerful than he actually is; the last thing he wants to do is burden Leon with his shit, Leon has enough of his own, and one thing Enrique does is try to limit how much he shows his true feelings to his friend.

"Hey, mon… how's it going?" Leon says in his cheery Jamaican accent, as he walks toward his friend, reaching his hand out to do their signature handshake.

"I'm doing good, bro… I'm doing good." Enrique says with a smile, shaking Leon's hand as he does.

Leon's eyes find Gabriela, Enrique's housekeeper, as she walks toward the door. He can't help but check her out, as she's wearing different clothes to her uniform today, as it's her day off. "Hey, G… how's it going?" He asks her with a smile.

"Great, thanks… forgot my wallet yesterday." She smiles, holding her wallet up. "Good job I figured this out before I went to the store."

"Uh, yeah... that would have been a nightmare," Leon says.

"Yeah, just a bit... got all my groceries to get today... would have been so embarrassing." She says. "I'd forget my head if it wasn't screwed on."

"I know the feeling," Leon says with sparkling eyes. He's always liked Gabriela, but over recent months, he's really taken a shine to her, and she looks incredible in what she's wearing today; a long green maxi dress and silver sandals, with her highlighted hair, styled in light waves.

Enrique catches Leon and Gabriela's vibe for a second and gives them a surprised smile. He would love nothing more than for the both of them to find love... they're both amazing people and deserve happiness... but he's not sure if either of them would ever act on their very obvious spark.

"Anyways... better get going," Gabriela says, pulling herself away from the situation. "The kids are in the car... better get on." She smiles. "Good to see you, Leon."

"Yeah... you, too," Leon says, not wanting to take his eyes off of her.

"I'll see you in the morning, Enrique." She says, as she walks toward the foyer.

"Yeah, see you tomorrow, G," Enrique says, before turning to Leon and saying quietly. "Bro... seriously?"

"What?" Leon says, looking all innocent.

"You two," Enrique whispers, as he watches Gabriela enter the elevator and the doors close.

"What about it?" Leon does his best to look confused; he knows exactly what Enrique is on about.

"What about it? Come on, papo... you know exactly what I'm on about...."

"I don't... we just talked... Jesus, Enrique... can I talk to somebody?" He smiles.

"Yeah... but I see it... and I just want you to know that I think it's nice... for the both of you."

"I don't know what you're talking about," Leon says. "Now, are you making me some coffee or what?"

"OK, OK," Enrique says, before turning and making his way to the kitchen with his friend. "The coffee is made."

Once Enrique has poured the coffee, they head up to the sun-drenched pool deck and sit out, enjoying the mid-morning rays, as they catch up; Enrique leaves the topic of Gabriela alone.

"So proud of you, bro," Enrique says, as he sips some of his cafécito. "Everything you're doing at the center... it's incredible... you were right... it's such a great thing for you to do... I can see you're benefitting from it... it's like, you were put on this earth to help people... you have a real way with people, you really do... I mean, I've always known that." He smiles. "Everybody at the center is super grateful... and so am I."

"Hey, mon... I want to thank you for the opportunity... you took a chance on me... and I'm super grateful... I understand your concerns... your worries... but seriously... it's so good for me... it helps me a lot... like, I get it... what these people are going through... I totally get it... and it's like, I don't know... it feels so good."

"I know... I can see that... it's like, it's easier for them to take advice from somebody who's been through it... who battles with this thing every day... it's like, the fact that you're going through the same as them, knocks down barriers... it's like they trust you immediately... the walls are down because they know that you know, how it feels."

"Thanks, mon... it means the world to hear you say that... I do my best... and I love it so much... it's like my work at the gym... it means so much to me that people trust me enough to help them... it takes a lot for them to do that."

"I know, papo... I know." Enrique agrees. He lights a cigar and tilts his face up to the sun for a couple of seconds as he exhales the smooth smoke; he's smoking way too much right now, and he knows it... but what can he do?

"So, how are you, mon? How's it all going?" Leon asks, approaching the subject with caution.

"I'm OK, ya know," Enrique says, fidgeting with the band of his cigar, looking awkward as hell; he really doesn't want to talk about what's going on with him right now, and he especially doesn't want to talk about it with Leon.

"You sure?" Leon asks with concern.

"Yeah, ya know... it's hard... the worst... but I'll be OK...." He says, looking at his friend, then taking another puff of his cigar before looking away and out to the view of the bay from the pool deck, ninety floors up above Brickell Avenue.

"I know, mon... it's the worst... I can see you're struggling." Leon says, taking a sip of his coffee.

"Yeah," Enrique says, tilting his head from side to side. "But what am I gonna do? The whole situation is fucked...." He takes another puff of his cigar and manages a sorrowful chuckle.

"And *I* fucked it... I fucked up the best thing I had in my life." He looks away again, feeling so ashamed of himself.

"You did the best you could... with it all, mon... don't beat yourself up about it... it's hard... grief... it's super hard to process... and when you suppress it... it only makes things worse...it manifests into every part of our lives." Leon regards his friend for a second before continuing. "You'll get through this, bro... I know you will... and you and Krissy will work this out... and at the end of the day... you don't need me telling you this... you already know it... but, once you open up to her... once you release all that pent-up hurt and pain... you'll feel like a different person... you will feel so free... so liberated... you'll feel on top of the world... it will clear the path for better things... and it will happen, it will... just give yourself a chance... it's been so long... you've been dealing with this in your own way, for as long as I can remember... nearly all your life... these things don't come easy, mon."

"I know," Enrique says, hating himself for even discussing this with Leon; he's more worried about his friend, than himself. "And I know, you know... more than anybody... you've been there... you're still there... I get it... and you're doing amazingly well, papo... the best... but me... I just keep on burying it... over and over... it's all I know... and now.... now it's like this huge fucking monster... and I can't fight it... it's so powerful."

"But you are… and you will win the battle."

"I hope so… all I can do, is hope… hope that I can get past this… hoping that Krissy will still be there when I do…."

"She will… I know she will." Leon says with certainty. He regards his friend once again before saying. "You taking care of yourself?"

"Yeah… why?" Enrique asks, trying his best to look confused at his friend's question.

"Well, I worry, ya know… I mean, you don't look like you've had a decent meal in weeks… you look tired… ya know… in the nicest possible way." Leon smiles, running his hand through his pristinely neat shoulder-length braids.

"Thanks, bro." Enrique manages a smile as he puts out his cigar, getting ready to light another. "Who needs enemies, huh?"

"I'm just being honest, bruh…." Leon chuckles. "But on the square… I worry…."

"I'm OK… guess, I've slipped off course a little… ya know."

"Well, I'm gonna make you some lunch," Leon says, getting up from his chair and picking up both of their empty coffee cups. "You stay here... get some sun... I'll be right back."

"Papo, you're not making me lunch... this is my house... I make *you* lunch." Enrique protests.

"I won't hear of it," Leon says. "Stay here... drink some water... you look like you could use some water." He smiles, knowing that Enrique has been hitting the bottle way too much recently. "And, try not to smoke yourself to death in my absence." He says, with raised eyebrows and a cheeky smile.

"Yeah, actually... I should give these a break." Enrique says, stubbing out the cigar he's just lit. He wants to cut back, and there's no time like the present.

Leon comes back up to the pool deck about twenty minutes later, carrying what could only be described as a banquet for just the two of them.

"Now, eat," Leon says, as he sits down at the table with his friend.

Enrique tucks into the amazing meal of healthy food Leon has prepared for them, and they talk a little about him and Kristie, mainly because Leon has led the conversation that way.

"I know what I have to do, but it's just so hard to reach," Enrique says. "It's so fucking hard, bro... you know what it's like."

"I get it... I really do... but you'll do it, mon... in time... one day, you'll wake up, and it will suddenly click into place, and you'll wonder what all the fuss was about." Leon says. "As they say, if it don't kill you, it will make you stronger." He smiles.

Enrique nods. Again, he knows that Leon knows this more than anybody, with what he's been through.

"You and Krissy will work it out, mon... you two are made for each other. You can't live without each other... and you won't... you'll be back together in no time... trust me."

"I wish I was as confident as you," Enrique says. And he does. He really wishes that he could believe that he could do what it takes to have his girl by his side again... that's all he wants... he knows he's fucked up... and he knows that he keeps fucking up... but he has to find some hope in his heart that he will find a way, what else is he to do? The alternative is too hard to even face.

* * *

Kristie

Mario and the girls are over at Kristie's apartment today, they're having a day of watching old movies, listening to music, and trying out different face masks and other beauty potions while sipping champagne in their pink silk pajamas.

After conversations about anything and everything, including Felicity's new man, the subject moves on to Kristie and Enrique's break up. As uncomfortable as Kristie feels about confiding in her friends about her and Enrique's situation, she has to talk to somebody, or she will go crazy... and she trusts these three wonderful people, more than anything in the world... the only other people she will discuss anything else with is her parents.

"So, how's things been, babe?" Lisa asks, as she tucks her platinum blonde hair behind her ear.

"Well, ya know... up and down," Kristie says, with a look of sadness on her beautiful face. "We argued the other night... I told him that maybe it's a good idea that we don't talk for a while... if at all... but we've worked things out... again... ya know." Kristie shakes her head; she knows that this is a cycle, when it comes to her and Enrique, and she has no idea how to break it. "I mean, I don't know... like, I know that perhaps I'm putting up with too much of his crap, but I love him so much, and I understand him... and I guess in some ways it's kind of easier to take while we're living apart, although I can't stand being apart from him, it's like I can... I dunno... it's like I can limit it, if that makes sense?"

"I totally get what you're saying," Lisa says. "It's like, you can have a break from it all while he's going through it all... like when you lived there, it was constant... whereas now he's getting it out of his system in a way... you can be there for him... but start to try and get on with things at the same time?"

"Yeah, that's right. It's like, we're not together... it's over...." Kristie says, as her voice begins to shake. "We are technically over... this is not a break... but I guess in a way, it could be viewed that way... because we've both expressed our desire to reconcile... it's something we both want so desperately, but I refuse to go back until he deals with his issues, or at least show signs of making progress with it all. Like, if I can see he's making changes... that's one thing... but I can't move back in until I see real changes. It kills me, it really does, and his behavior... sometimes I wonder why I'm even speaking to him... and that's why I told him the other night that I don't want to speak to him for a while... like, things escalate so quickly... we seem to go zero, to like a thousand, in a nanosecond... he just flies off the handle... I mean, I know that's just his nature... he's so impulsive... so unpredictable... and I must admit, it's something that attracts me to him... like, I love that he's so impulsive... so unpredictable... but the downside to it is, he's like it when things get bad, too... and that's not so great." She says with a sad smile. "But, I understand him... I understand his mind... and I know he's only lashing out because he's trying to deal with all this... with his issues... and I know how frustrated he is that he can't...."

"Totally get it, babe," Felicity says. "It must be so hard for you both... and we hate to see you this way... the both of you... but he will do this... he loves you so, so much... he worships you... he doesn't need to say anything... it's so obvious by the way he even looks at you... he's always making sure you have everything you need... that everything is taken care of. He's so attentive and loving... it's just such a shame that things have to be this way."

Kristie begins to sob. Everything her friend is saying is true. Enrique *is* all of those things. He always makes sure she's OK and takes care of everything. But sadly, he has a lot of issues. As she always says, he's a good man with a lot of issues. And if those issues can be at least dealt with a tiny bit, things between them would be so much easier.

"It's OK, babe... don't get upset," Mario says. "This is not worth your tears, my darling... this is only temporary. It's not for long, and you will be back together... and more in love than ever."

"You will, babe... I just know you will." Felicity says, as all four friends form a group hug.

"It's all gonna be just fine," Lisa says. "It will all work out... trust us."

They all hold their hug for a while longer, and then as they separate, Mario says to Kristie, "You need to eat, babe... you haven't even eaten the chocolate I brought along, and you love chocolate."

"I know, babe... and you brought my favorites," Kristie says, wiping her tears. "Chocolate's always been my downfall... but I'm in no mood for food lately."

"Well, you must eat," Mario says. "You have to stay healthy... perhaps chocolate isn't the best thing... I will make you some pasta... how about that, baby? You love my pasta."

"I do," Kristie replies with a smile.

"Well, ladies," Mario says, brimming with exuberance. "This bitch is gonna cook us some of her mean pasta... I thought I could get this queen to eat, by bringing her favorite chocolate... but it would seem that I will have to force-feed her some pasta, instead." He jokes.

The three ladies all laugh.

"Can't wait," Felicity says, full of enthusiasm.

"Me neither," Lisa adds.

"You're so sweet, babe," Kristie says, knowing that right now, for the first time in her life, she probably will have to force down Mario's amazingly decadent pasta... but he's right... she needs to eat.

"Anything for you, baby," Mario says sweetly, before heading to the kitchen and checking out what ingredients Kristie has. "Well, you have pasta... so that's a start." He says, before opening the refrigerator. "But not much else." He says in Spanish, as his eyes scan the fridge. "Looks like I'll be going to the store... I'll go get dressed... can't walk the streets dressed in pink silk pajamas." He chuckles.

"You could pull it off." Kristie manages a joke, for which she surprises herself with.

"I probably could," Mario says, full of drunken enthusiasm. "But, this bitch is married now, and I can't have all the boys flocking to me, now, can I? I have to be respectable!"

They all laugh.

"Shall we come with you?" Kristie asks, as they all continue their conversation in Spanish.

"No, you ladies stay here... I'll go get the things I need, and I'll be right back in a jiffy." He says, heading to the bedroom to get changed.

"You're such a beautiful person," Kristie says, full of appreciation. "Thank you for this, babe."

"Any time, my love," Mario replies, before getting changed and heading to the shop.

A while later, once the pasta is cooked, they all sit out on the balcony and eat the delicious Italian cuisine Mario has made with so much love; it's delicious, as always.

They chat some more, flowing between English and Spanish as they talk about anything and everything.

"Your Spanish," Mario says to Kristie, with a huge smile beaming on his handsome face. "So beautiful... incredible... I remember when you couldn't even speak a word... well, aside from hello and goodbye."

Kristie smiles. This is true; Kristie has always been ashamed that she could never pick up Spanish, especially as she was born and raised in Miami, and she even studied it at school... she's never been very good at languages... until she met Enrique. "Well, we have Enrique Cruz to thank for that." She says, as she raises a sad smile.

"And he taught you beautifully," Mario says, reaching for Kristie's hand and holding it across the table.

"Thanks, babe." She smiles, as she holds his hand back.

Mario changes tac; he can see that Kristie is getting upset again, and he wants her to feel better. "I know; why don't we go shopping to Sawgrass Mills." He suggests, as they continue to eat their dinner. "Ya know, sing along to Beyoncé in the car, all the way there and back." He says, full of enthusiasm. "All us queens... with Queen Bey along for the ride! How about it?"

They all agree.

"I'm never one to miss out on a bargain." Lisa giggles.

"I know." Kristie agrees. "We haven't done this for so long." Perhaps the retail therapy will be good for her? Hopefully, it will pull her out of her depression, although she doesn't hold out much hope. There's only one thing that will pull her out of this misery, and that's being back in Enrique's arms, but sadly, right now, that's completely impossible.

* * *

Enrique

That evening, after doing some work in the office and then calling Leon, Enrique finds himself reading about the new President of Cuba. He shakes his head as he reads a couple of articles; he really can't see things changing any time soon, even with this new guy in charge of his beloved island.

When Castro took over the island back in the 50s, people say that it was like a jewel, with a bright future ahead of it... it was thriving, and now it's anything but. What was once beautiful streets brimming with glorious architecture, full of glamour and grace, has now fallen into utter disrepair and is crumbling with decay; it's a very sad sight to see. Sadly, the Havana everybody sees in the pictures has disintegrated beyond measure, and some of the city doesn't even exist anymore, it's just rubble. The term "fallen into disrepair" would be generous, at best, when it comes to describing Cuba's architecture and infrastructure.

What he feels for the most, is the people... they're suffering... the poverty is heartbreaking, the food and medical shortages, the housing... the repression... everything... and it kills him that he can't do anything to help... he would fix all of this in a heartbeat, as well as restore and rebuild the island back to its original glory... but sadly, his hands are tied.

Cuba is only ninety miles away from American shores, yet it could be a million miles away, as far as Enrique is concerned. Until it's free, he will never step foot in his beloved homeland, just like his father and the rest of his family. They have no surviving relatives there, so there is no desperate need for them to be reunited with their loved ones, like many who live in Miami and across the United States.

Right now, to Enrique, Cuba feels just like that… a million miles away, but he has hope in his heart that one day, he will get to walk the beautiful streets of Havana and Cienfuegos, where his father was born. His mother's side of the family is from Havana, and his father's side is from Cienfuegos, which is on the south coast.

With this age of social media and the internet, although very closely monitored, Enrique can see things changing at some point, as people can now see a whole new world that's out there, and they want to be part of it. Before this, they were more accepting as they didn't know any better.

With that being said, Enrique knows that no matter how much you think that somebody new in power will make a difference, he doesn't have much faith that things will improve in the near future; as his father, José, has said many times… they're all the same, and he agrees… and this is why he will always vote one way or the other, not because he's hugely into politics, or believes any of them are amazing, by any stretch… and yes, he keeps up to speed, but he's not one for debating the issue, or even choosing sides, although, of course, he is against communism… but when he votes, he votes for who he thinks is the best at the time for his beliefs, and what he feels America needs at that moment… but the main reason is because his father taught him the importance of voting from an early age. José said, "In Cuba... you don't have a choice who will be president... the decision is made for you... the people don't have a say. You have to make the most of a privilege, such as the right to vote, especially when you're from a country like Cuba." And due to those lessons, Enrique will always vote, taking advantage of his right as an American citizen, something he's super proud of, just like his Cuban heritage, too.

As he reads through some press reports online, he remembers the many conversations he's had with Kristie about Cuba. Although she is of British heritage, Kristie loves Cuban history and the culture, and this was way before she even met Enrique. When they went for a walk together the first night they met, she told him all about her fascination with the island and all things Cuban; he smiles as he remembers him being hopeful that it was a good sign that she accidently said she was obsessed with anything Cuban, especially as he is just that... Cuban!

He recalls one conversation in particular.

"I would love to go, babe... when it's free... I would love to go with you." She said to him, full of enthusiasm and excitement, just like many times before. "It would be so special, as I know what a free Cuba would mean to you... to your father... your whole family... it will be a beautiful day when it comes... and it will... I know it will!"

"It will… and mami, when that day comes… we will celebrate like crazy… and then we'll go straight there… to the island… where we can stroll hand in hand through the majestic streets of Havana, then along the Malecón… then go celebrate some more with some mojitos at the Hotel Nacional, followed by dinner and dancing at The Trop… it will be a dream come true, baby… you and me, and beautiful Cuba… it will happen… I just know it will." He said, sounding all dreamy and hopeful, and in some ways he still is… not just for a free Cuba… but that one day, he will get to take Kristie there… not just to see the sights, to experience the culture and beautiful island, but to visit the places his family used to live and work… they've been to Madrid, a trip Kristie so generously surprised him with last year, and visited where some of his family lived and run a farm… how magical would it be to do the same in Cuba… and if he can, that really will be a dream come true!

As he finishes the article, Kristie calls him, and to his delight, things are sweet between them. He checks in on her, and she's doing OK, which he's happy about after what happened not only between them, but with Peter, too.

They talk a tiny bit about what's happening in Cuba and then onto what they've been up to today. Their whole conversation is in Spanish, but flows into English from time to time… nothing new there… just like most people in and around Miami.

"Aww, ya know, your voice is so beautiful when you speak Spanish." He smiles.

"Enrique," Kristie says shyly; she's been speaking Spanish for years now, but still gets shy when Enrique comments on it.

"What?" He says with surprise. "You know how much I love to hear you speak Spanish... it's beautiful."

"I love to hear you speak it too, babe... I always have... it's very sexy." She replies, forgetting their situation for a second and feeling back in their groove again. "Besides... I can only speak Spanish because of you... when we met, I could barely speak a word... terrible, considering I was born and raised in Miami."

He smiles at the memory of helping her learn Spanish; she was such a quick study, although she'll never let him tell her that. "I remember hearing you speak Spanish at La Caretta once." He says. "And I remember thinking about how beautiful you sounded... it was so...." He stops himself from saying what he's about to say. He feels it's inappropriate.

"Bad?" Kristie tries to finish off his sentence.

"No baby... absolutely not." He says, remembering the moment like it was yesterday. "You know how

I feel about you speaking Spanish... and that particular time was no different... even though we still hadn't spoken at that point."

"Oh, right... yes... I see." Kristie says, going quiet for a moment.

"I'm sorry, baby... I shouldn't have brought it up... it was wrong of me." He says softly. "I should know better... I just... I don't know... it's like I forget... I mean, I never forget... but it's like when we talk... it's like we're still us... we're still you and me."

"I know... I know exactly what you mean... don't worry... it's OK... I understand."

After the call, he sits alone, sipping some rum with a cigar on the pool deck. He finds himself writing another text to Kristie to tell her that he misses her. Then, the same thoughts from last night and all the other nights enter his mind, making him think about the message he's about to send. Is it wise? Is it fair on her? Is it the right thing to do? No, no, it's not.

He deletes the text once again, then places his cell down on the table in front of him, and looks up to the starry sky above him, letting out a long slow breath. "Please God, help me." He whispers. "Please."

Chapter 14
Wednesday, May 2nd, 2018
Kristie's Birthday

After waking alone and devastated on her birthday, Kristie answers the intercom; it's one of the doormen, Cedric... he has a delivery for her. She asks him to bring it up for her. As she opens the door, all she can see is a wall of white roses; as soon as she sees the bouquet, she knows exactly who they're from... Enrique.

She thanks Cedric as he places the vase down on the white marble breakfast bar and tips him. Once the doorman has left her apartment, she reaches into the bouquet of one hundred of the best quality white roses and finds the card.

She opens the envelope and reads the white card inside.

Dearest Kristie,
Happy birthday!
I hope your day is as special as you are.
All my love forever and always,
Enrique
xxxxx

Kristie bursts into tears; she has to speak to him... she has to hear his voice.

She finds her cell, which is on the breakfast bar, and calls him, trying to gather herself in the process.

"Hey." She says quietly, as he answers.

"Hey, baby... happy birthday." He says softly; he can hear in her voice that she's been crying.

"Thank you... thank you for the flowers." She says. "They're so beautiful."

"You're so welcome... I... I... uhh... I wanted to send you something... it just didn't feel right not to... although I know things are the way they are between us." He pauses before continuing. "I... uhh.... I hope it's OK... ya know... that I sent you them."

"Of course, babe... of course it is... they're beautiful... absolutely beautiful."

"That's OK, then." He raises a relieved smile. Kristie asked him to stop sending the roses he used to send her every Monday, once she left; it was too painful for her to keep receiving them, but as it was her birthday, he wanted to send her something, and he's glad he did the right thing by sending them. "How are you, darling?" He asks. "How's your morning been so far?"

"It's been OK, ya know." She says, trying to hide her true feelings of waking up alone on her birthday... something she didn't used to get upset about before she met Enrique, but now it feels so tragic. Every birthday since she's been with him has been so magical, and now, here she is... alone... alone without him... the love of her life.

As her thoughts float through her mind, suddenly, she becomes overwhelmed with emotion and bursts into tears again.

"Oh, baby... oh, no, baby," Enrique says quickly, full of concern and heartbreak; he hates to hear her cry.

"Oh, Enrique." She sobs. "I hate this... I hate it all... I don't want any of it... all I want is us... you and me... and I can't have that... we can't be together... I'm alone... alone without you... and I can't bear it... waking up without you for the first time on my birthday... after the last three years... you made my birthdays so special... so beautiful... and now... here I am... here... without you... without you to kiss me when I wake...." Her voice trails off.

As Enrique listens to Kristie sob and sob, as she tries to get her words out... each word as it leaves her lips, is like a burning stake through his heart. With his hand to his mouth, his blue eyes flood with tears; he can't speak... he can't breathe. You did this! He tells himself. You did this! Now, sort your fucking shit out!

"I'm sorry," Kristie says, as she heaves through her tears. "The last thing you want is to hear me having a meltdown when you're at work... you have more important things to deal with."

"Shall I come over... I want to be with you... to hold you... to hold you until your tears stop... until the pain stops." He says quickly... he has to do something to help her. He's the reason why this most beautiful girl is in so much pain, and the least he can do is be there for her.

"I would love to... but we can't... it's not a good idea." She says, drying her eyes; even though she feels the way she does and knows that being in Enrique's arms right now is all she needs, the relief will be short-lived, nothing has changed between them; he's still the same... he still hasn't made any headway on dealing with his issues.

"I understand." He says, his words are barely audible. He closes his eyes, forcing his tears away. He feels like absolute shit, so much so, he feels like he's dying inside. For a second, he considers driving over there anyway, as he's so worried about her, but he knows he has to protect her from him and the pain he keeps causing her. He wants nothing more than to drive over to her apartment and spend the day with her, any way he can... even if it's just to sit with her; he would be the happiest man alive... but he has to do what's best for her. She deserves what he can't give her, and that is peace.

"Thank you." She whispers. "And I'm sorry."

"There's no need to thank me... and there's absolutely no need to apologize."

"But I know you have so much going on, right now... meetings... deadlines... everything... the last thing you need is me, bawling my eyes out, down the phone to you, when all you did was send me some flowers." She manages a tiny giggle.

"Baby, I'm here for you anytime, you know that... everything else can wait." He says meaning every word of it. He knows he has a boardroom full of people waiting for him, but he really doesn't give a fuck.

"Yeah, but it's not right that I keep you from your work."

"You're not keeping me from anything... besides... this is all my doing... and I can't tell you how terrible this makes me feel... seeing you this way... it kills me, babe... I'm so sorry... for everything... I'm so, so sorry...."

Kristie stays quiet, listening to his words. He sounds absolutely broken, just like her. "I know." She manages with a whisper.

"I'm so, so sorry." He whispers again, looking out of the floor-to-ceiling window toward her building; his need to be with her is so desperate, it's a physical pain, and there's nothing he can do to ease it... well, nothing in his power, anyway.

"I know you are... I really do, babe." She whispers, sniffling as she calms.

"What are you going to do today?" He asks softly; he's almost hopeful that she might change her mind and ask him to meet her.

"I'm going to mom and dad's for dinner... just a quiet one... just me, mom, and dad... I don't feel up to much else."

Enrique nods. As if his heart isn't breaking enough, it's just smashed to pieces once again, as he thinks about the sorry situation, a sorry situation that he caused... him and his shit. "That sounds nice." He says, sounding a little more upbeat; he's doing his best to be strong for Kristie.

"Yeah." She manages, before saying. "I guess I'd better let you get back to it... you have a lot to do today, what with being in New York yesterday... I just wanted to say thank you for the flowers... it was a lovely thought."

"You're so welcome, baby." He smiles.

They say their goodbyes, and Enrique sits for a few moments, looking out at Kristie's building, while he gathers himself ready for this meeting, he's about to chair.

With his game face firmly on, he says to himself. "Back to the grind, papo." He takes a deep breath. "You got this... you've fucking got this!"

* * *

Kristie

After driving over to her parent's house on Sunset Island, listening to Beyoncé's "I Miss You" over and over again, Kristie is greeted warmly by her mom and dad. She cries as they hold her. She's so thankful that she has such amazing parents. she may only have a small family, but there's a whole lot of love to go around.

As she sits at the table on the terrace of her parent's bayfront home, lost in thoughts about her and Enrique, she glances over to the pool and remembers him singing Frank Sinatra to her on the stage that hovered over the pool, at her very glamorous birthday party last year. Tears fill her eyes as she remembers such a magical time, back when things were so much happier. She was standing near where the stage was, right in front of where she's sitting now; as she casts her mind back, she knows that she would never have imagined that she would be in this situation a year later, sitting here with her parents by herself, because that's all she can handle today.

She looks down at the platinum Cartier Love bracelet Enrique gifted her when they first got together. As she runs her thumb over the precious metal, precious in more ways than one, she thinks to herself that she doesn't feel that she could ever take it off. It's been fastened on her wrist ever since the day Enrique put it on her, and she will wear it forever... it's so special to her... they might not be together anymore, but she can't bring herself to even think about removing something so meaningful to her... it will stay fixed on her wrist forever... just like her love for Enrique... it will be with her for the rest of her life.

* * *

After saying goodbye to her mom and dad, Kristie comes home to find several bouquets of flowers and presents from Enrique's family wishing her a happy birthday. She bursts into tears as she reads each and every card.

Her cell vibrates in her Birken, and she reaches her hand inside her bag and finds her phone. It's a text from Enrique.

How was your
day, my darling?
xxxxx

It was good,
thanks, babe.

How about you?
I have so many
beautiful flowers
and gifts from the
family. So sweet.
xxxxx

My day was good,
thanks, baby.
Aww, that's so
nice.
Xxxxx

I know.
xxxxx

Kristie is trying to sound upbeat, after their telephone conversation earlier, she doesn't want to keep putting on him... at the end of the day, she knows he has his own feelings to deal with regarding this too. She makes a mental note to send all the family thank you cards tomorrow, before saying good night to Enrique and crying herself to sleep again, cuddling up to Enrique's pillow, missing him more than ever.

* * *

Enrique

Enrique feels like shit that he's not spending Kristie's birthday with her, plus, to make matters worse, tomorrow marks the anniversary of the first day he ever saw her walking down Ocean Drive.

He misses his girl like crazy. She's been gone a month now, and it feels like a lifetime. He's a broken man and has no clue what to do to fix himself. He had business meetings up in New York the other day, and one was a dinner. Under normal circumstances, he would have stayed at the New York apartment, but he couldn't bring himself to. He and Kristie have made so many happy memories up there, he couldn't face it, just like the homes in Beverly Hills, Aspen, and The Bahamas; he doesn't think he could ever return to any of them and has even considered selling them all, even Manatee, but his father advised him not to make any rash decisions, at least not when things are so raw.

As he sits and reminisces about him and his girl together at all the different houses, he remembers her massaging him in front of the log fire up in New York. It was a freezing cold day, and they stayed in and made love for most of the day, sipping hot cocoa and falling in and out of sleep together; it was such a beautiful day... they had so many days like this.

Kristie's delicate hands were so soothing and made him relax in ways he never knew he could; she had a way of making him feel at peace... she gave him a sense of comfort he craves for so badly right now, a sense of comfort he chose not to see or feel during the last few months of their relationship... something he deeply regrets.

As his mind replays him then massaging her beautiful body, as she lay naked, on top of a blanket, in front of the fire, he envisages every inch of her silky skin, as it ripples beneath his fingertips; every detail of her glorious curves are memorized in his mind... he remembers every single millimeter of her delicious figure... every curve, every *thing*... all of her... he will never forget her... he might not have seen her for an entire month, but the image of Kristie Carrington... the epitome of perfection, is well and truly burned into his mind... and he has no trouble seeing her delectable body... her graceful and extremely feminine figure, in his mind... her dark brown eyes... her voluminous brunette hair... so long, it skimmed just above her waist... her beautiful face with high cheekbones, and her full lips... the feel of her silky, tanned skin... he remembers everything about this most incredible lady, and he will never, ever forget her.

His mind might be all over the place, but one thing he does know... one thing he's always known is... he loves Kristie more than anything in the world... he always has, and he always will... he's crazy about her... he's crazy about everything about her... the way she talks... especially when she speaks Spanish... the way she sings and dances, fooling around... he's crazy about her walk... everything... he could watch her forever... he could never get enough of watching her curves sway as she walked, especially in her Louboutin's.

He sits on the balcony just before midnight, with a cigar and some rum, listening to Otis Redding's "These Arms of Mine" over and over again, looking out over the bay, thinking about how magical last year was when they had the beautiful party at her parents.

He finds himself looking through photos of the two of them together at the party... they looked so elegant and so in love; he was dressed in his white tuxedo and black bow tie, Kristie looked absolutely incredible wearing her white flapper-style fringe mini dress, which was saturated in beads, crystals, and sequins, along with four-inch silver Jimmy Choo sandals; she looked sensational... she always does.

As he flicks through the pictures, he sees one of him up on stage with his father, Leon, Sánchez, and García, as well as Kristie's dad, Jon. He smiles as he remembers them singing Rat Pack songs like they were the very Rat Pack themselves! His smile widens as he remembers seeing Kristie's beautiful smile, as she watches him sing. Enrique hates the thought of getting on stage and singing... but his friends always persuade him to... and once he's up there... he loves it... he must admit.

His smile suddenly is replaced with a solemn expression, as he then remembers singing "The

Way You Look Tonight" by Frank Sinatra to Kristie, and how she cried with happiness at his thoughtful gesture. He misses her so damn much... why did he have to ruin it all? Why did he have to do what he did to her? Why can't he fix things? Why can't they go back to the way they were? He is heartbroken beyond belief... devastated, and heartbroken... he is a broken man... shattered to pieces, and so completely desperate to have his girl in his arms again.

Chapter 15
Thursday, May 3rd, 2018

Today marks the anniversary of the day Enrique first saw Kristie. He feels sick to the stomach, drowning in torment and devastation... he feels dead inside as he recalls what happened on this very day, four years ago... a day when his whole world turned upside down, and he fell head over heels in love with the most beautiful lady in the world... he fell so in love with her, that he knows he will never love, ever again.

They had, and he knows they still have, a connection that compares to nothing else... it's so strong and powerful, and he knows that this is the reason why Kristie has said that they can't see each other. She doesn't need to say anything; Enrique just knows... and she's right. Their connection is something that the two of them will never be able to fight against or resist... and to see each other would only put them both in a situation that would pull them back together, as it's so magnetic... it's indescribable... it's beyond anything sexual... it's more than love, too... it's something else that cannot be put into words... Lord knows they've tried!

As much as he wants nothing more than to be with her, especially on a day like today, he respects her wishes, and he knows it's sensible, as he knows that even with a connection like theirs, there is way more to making a relationship work. He has to sort out his mind once and for all, to avoid repeating the same mistakes again... he can't put Kristie through anymore... he's put her through so much already... he loves her more than anything, and she deserves the best version of him, not the selfish, angry, frustrated drunk, she was getting toward the end of their relationship.

As he thinks of him and Kristie together and the way she made him feel, he shakes his head with disbelief; Christ, she is so beautiful and so intoxicating. He sometimes used to wonder if he would survive the dizzy heights of carnal ecstasy he would reach when he was with her. When they made love, they made love on another level to anything he had ever experienced before in his life, and he was addicted, and still is. He could never love anybody again, and he certainly could never be with anybody else... after Kristie, nothing would ever compare.

Before he met Kristie, for the most part, Enrique steered well clear of the opposite sex, as every time he got involved with them, his life would become a complete mess, although he does have a bit of a past, it's nothing that would put him in the same category of his friends, Sánchez and García. Enrique's take on women and sex is very different from his dear friends, but each to their own. When Enrique was growing up, his father drummed into his head that women are not to be objectified... they are to be respected, however, that didn't stop him from dabbling in the same lifestyle as his friends for a period of time.

Yes, Enrique has had his moments when it comes to women, and he went through a phase that some might describe as him going around the block a bit, but he learned very quickly that that kind of lifestyle wasn't for him. Yes, he's had one-night stands, and yes, he's been on dates with various women, and he's had a few relationships, which all turned out to be complete disasters. Then he met Kristie, and it was like they were made for each other in ways he could never imagine.

Aside from the love they share... a love that is so deep, it's indescribable, they also brought out sides to each other they never knew existed and enjoyed experimenting with different things in the bedroom, and Enrique loved every minute of it. There was no judgment, no boundaries, and no limits... just the two of them exploring different sides of themselves.

When they made love, it was always such an extreme version of intense, it was primal and raw, and at times, animalistic, even... it was like they were starved for each other, and when they finally connected, they had to get as close to each other as they could... they couldn't get enough of each other to the point where it didn't matter where they were, all they had to do was look at each other, and within seconds they were somewhere away from prying eyes, surrendering to their body's needs... needs that made it so difficult for them to resist.

It was so passionate between them, it was on fire, but most of all, it was always love... overwhelmingly consuming, deeply core-shaking love, a love that has made sure that he will never, ever be the same again after he first laid eyes on the most beautiful lady in the world... the love of his life... Kristie Carrington.

He closes his eyes and relives the beautiful moment when he first saw her walking down Ocean Drive four years ago today... four years ago, his life changed forever. He remembers everything about that twenty-second encounter like it was yesterday, hell, he replayed it over and over in his mind a trillion times after it happened. He remembers wondering how on earth he could be so affected by seeing someone for only a few seconds... how the hell could his whole world be turned upside down by seeing this lady, this most incredibly beautiful lady, walk past him while chatting to her friend, and not even have a clue about his existence; to her, he was invisible.

In his mind's eye, he sees the vision of beauty that was Kristie Carrington, dressed in his favorite color ... cobalt blue... her dress was long and floating in the breeze, and she was wearing her silver Jimmy Choo sandals, four inches high... so elegant... so sexy. Her long brunette hair was cascading down her back, styled in loose curls, and she was wearing silver-mirrored aviators... she looked an absolute dream... and she knocked him off his feet... he had no clue what was happening to him... until one day, it dawned on him... he had fallen truly, madly and very, very deeply in love with this brunette beauty... and that love will last forever... until the end of time.

* * *

Saturday, May 5th, 2018

After much persuasion, Kristie goes out with her friends to a club on South Beach; they tie it in with celebrating Cinco de Mayo on Española Way, a pretty tree-lined Spanish street adorned with pink colonial architecture, reminiscent of Mediterranean villages.

It's 3am, and they've just left the club on South Beach. With their arms linked, all four more than tipsy friends walk back down Española Way toward Washington Avenue, talking about Kristie's breakup with Enrique.

"As frustrated as I get and at times... as angry as I get with him," Kristie says. "All I want is him... all I want is us... I will never stop loving him... he's the love of my life... like, I can't even describe to you guys how much I love him... it's like, on some crazy level... it's so intense, and the love I feel from him is just as powerful... I know he's lost... and I know I can't help him find his way, but I'll wait for him... I will wait for him as long as it takes."

"Aww babe... that's so sweet," Lisa says. "You two are so cute, I've always loved you together. From that very first time I saw you together in Liv, I knew you would be together forever... I just knew it. It was so obvious, wasn't it, Flick?"

"Yeah... like totally," Felicity says. "You could feel the love between you. It was crazy... like, it was like there was this kind of spark that ignited, and you could almost see it... it was crazy how intense it was. You two are so meant to be together, babe, just look at this as part of your journey... try not to look at it as this terrible thing... try to look at it as a blip... a blip that will lead you to better things... like, imagine when it was good... well, imagine it being way better than that... imagine you being in a way better place with a stronger love... a more open... a more powerful love... imagine that."

"Exactly, babe," Mario says. "It's gonna happen very soon, my darling, I just know it. These things take time, so please try to have patience. I know it's so hard for you right now... so painful... but it will be worth it when you're on the other side... trust me, baby... trust me."

"Aww, thanks, guys... you really are the best friends I could ever ask for." Kristie says. "And I will wait for him... no matter how hard it gets... I know this is all part of the process... I know him snapping and lashing out is only because he's hurting... like mom said, hurt people, hurt people... and I know that's what's happening here... he's only lashing out the way he is because he's in so much pain... although it's so hard when he does... this man is usually so kind and gentle... but he does have a temper and a mean tongue at times."

"Don't we all, don't we all," Mario says. "At the end of the day, there is no excuse for it, but we all act in less than favorable ways when we're going through shit... my Gustavo has suffered the wrath of my mean tongue at times, and let me tell you, ladies, I'm not proud... but I'm Italian... what can I say!"

They all laugh.

"But Enrique is Cuban... not a lot of difference." Mario continues. "We're both very passionate... and when we fight or get angry... we fight and get angry in a passionate way... not always a great outcome... but we don't mean it... I mean, Gustavo is an exception to the rule, being Argentinian, you'd expect the same, you'd think he'd be fanning the flames... you'd expect massive explosions every time we fight... but no... he's the... the extinctioner."

The girls all burst out laughing.

"Extinguisher," Felicity says.

"Oh, yes. Extingtinc... how you say it?" Mario asks.

"Ex ting uish er," Felicity says.

"Ex tincgk...." Mario tries again.

"Extinguisher." Felicity repeats, "Ex ting uisher."

"Ex tingkt wish...."

"No." Felicity giggles along with the other girls in a tipsy, girly fashion. "Extinguisher."

"Ex tingkwitcher?"

"NO!!"

"Oh, fuck it!!!" Mario says, waving his hand dismissively. "English is a stupid language anyways!"

They all laugh out loud.

As they continue down the street, still giggling, one of the many secret walkways along the pretty Mediterranean-style street adorned with pink bougainvillea and pink-painted architecture, catches Kristie's eye. She remembers walking along this very street with Enrique so many times, but one time stands out in her mind, right now... they were singing 80s songs as they staggered down the street arm in arm, giggling like crazy fools as they did.

They just came out of the same club she went to with her friends tonight, and were a little worse for wear. She remembers dragging him to this very passageway and making mad, passionate love to him, as he pinned her up against the wall, giving her everything she wanted and needed.

She feels sadness in her heart as she thinks of another one of their many happy memories. It might be sordid and leud to some, but to Kristie, it's another happy, beautiful memory of the two of them, loving each other in one of the many ways they did. They had such a powerful connection, so beautiful and raw, yet so tender and gentle, and she misses everything about it... she misses her man so much... she misses everything about him... why do things have to be this way? Why can't they just figure things out and move on together?

She pulls Lisa and Felicity closer to her as she continues to walk down the pretty street painted in pink, and prays that one day she will get to relive those happy memories with her man, the love of her life, again.

* * *

As she enters her apartment, once again, she wishes Enrique was here with her. She considers calling him as she wonders if he will still be awake, which is a possibility, but she doesn't want to disturb him, just in case he isn't.

As she lays alone in bed, she cuddles up to his pillow and can't help but remember the many times she's come home to Enrique a little on the intoxicated side and how adorable he finds it. She manages a tiny smile at the memory, as she remembers coming home from her work Christmas party at 3am, and how she sang "Drunk in Love" by Beyoncé to him while dancing around the great room suggestively, grinding up against her man, teasing him to the point of insanity. Then, just as he thought he was about to explode, she began singing "Partition," and just like Beyoncé in the video for this song, she did a little performance for Enrique... full of confidence, like she was one of the professional dancers, at Crazy Horse in Paris.

Enrique stood and watched with a surprised, sexy smile and raised eyebrows, as Kristie was dancing around the great room and clambering all over the sofa, seducing him as she tried out her Crazy Horse dance moves on the sofa, nearly killing herself in the process.

Enrique couldn't take his eyes off of her. His smile kept widening the longer the performance went on, and he was loving every minute of it... and he didn't hold back telling her either!

"You're so fucking sexy, ya know that?" He said, as he stood looking all tall, dark, and muscly, with one arm across his torso, as he ran his forefinger back and forth across his lower lip, in the way he always does when he's contemplating what he's going to do to her.

"You like, Mr. Cruz?" She asked him as she began a striptease, for his eyes only. Even with her being so drunk and cute... it was so erotic and seductive... she gave him no choice but to pick her up and carry her upstairs, where they had the wildest of sex all night.

To this day, Kristie still shocks herself with how extroverted she became with Enrique. It was like he gave her the confidence to do anything she wanted, and when she'd had a few drinks, that confidence was only magnified by what felt like a thousand times over. She shakes her head as she remembers herself parading around the living area like she was on stage at the famous cabaret club in Paris. This was something she would never have done before she met him... he made her feel like she could do anything, even be a professional dancer, it would seem!

Kristie has the best memories of her life with Enrique, and it breaks her heart that they can't be together, especially during such a special time like her birthday. She hates every minute of being apart from him... she feels so lonely and broken without him. She tries to comfort herself with more happy memories, like when she came home one night from work, and Sting and The Police were blaring through the penthouse, and Enrique was singing along to the music at the top of his voice. As he belted out the lyrics to "Every Little Thing She Does Is Magic", he didn't even notice that Kristie was there watching him; she couldn't get enough... it was so funny, yet sexy as hell.

So many of her memories of her relationship with Enrique are surrounded by music... it was such a huge part of their lives, and it still is. All she seems to do is listen to music right now, although she tries to avoid songs that remind her of memories too painful to relive at the moment, like "Tu Amor Me Hace Bien" by Marc Anthony, a song that they decided was theirs, very early on in their relationship.

With visions of her man dancing around the penthouse to Sting and The Police, like nobody's watching, Kristie somehow manages to fall asleep as she cuddles up to what used to be his pillow, reminiscing of happier times with the man she misses and adores so much. He's such a good man... the best... but he has a lot of issues that were making her life intolerable, but she loves him so damn much. Why does life have to be so cruel?

* * *

Sunday, May 6th, 2018
Kristie

As the sun begins to rise, Kristie decides to go for a run along the beach at the southern tip of South Beach, where her apartment is located; she's desperate to clear her mind after yet another sleepless night. She's sick and tired of always being sick and tired. She's all for feeling your emotions and facing them, but this is ridiculous, she can't carry on like this forever. She has to find a way to live her life without Enrique, somehow. She would do anything to go back and make things work, but he's not showing any signs of getting any better, sadly. She can't spend her entire life feeling this way.

As her feet pound the sand, she's listening to her John Newman playlist on blast through her AirPods; the very playlist she used to listen to with Enrique. As she runs along the shoreline of the sugar-white beach, she glances out at the aquamarine ocean as it glistens in the sunrise; the sky is so beautiful, and she forces herself to appreciate how lucky she really is to live in such a beautiful city. She may be in agonizing pain right now, she might be desperately heartbroken, but she's trying to heal, and gratitude is a good place to start.

As she listens to a mix of uplifting dance tracks, she remembers all the good times they shared, listening to not only John Newman but also all the other music they listened to together. Music was such a huge part of their life as a couple. She smiles as she visualizes Enrique singing various songs to her, belting out the lyrics like he's the very singer himself. He loves to sing, and he's quite the performer, too, not that he will ever admit it.

He used to complain like crazy about getting up on the stage in karaoke bars or at parties when his friends would ask him to join them, but as soon as he was up there, he loved every single minute of it. Kristie manages a giggle to herself, so many fun memories float through her mind as she keeps running along the shore.

As one of her favorite songs, "Something Special" plays through her AirPods, she becomes overwhelmed with emotion, and she can't help but allow her tears to fall as she thinks back to the amazing memories she shared with Enrique... her handsome Cuban... the love of her life... and although she might not be with him, right now... they might be apart... but she will forever hold their happy memories in her heart... no matter how low she feels, no matter how difficult things get, she will always have the best times of her life with her, and for that she will be grateful to him forever.

* * *

Enrique

Enrique is sitting in the all-cream and rich dark wood great room at his father's mansion on Star Island. It's a rainy afternoon; the weather is dark and miserable... just like Enrique.

They discuss the break up and the fact that it was Kristie's birthday on Wednesday... Enrique hates himself for not spending it with her... "Up until this past week or so, all I seem to do is cause arguments with her... and she doesn't deserve that... she doesn't deserve any of it." He says to his father.

"You're deflecting your shit onto her." José says. "And you have to get that under control, papi... you'll only drive her further away... you have to stop this... it's doing neither of you any good... talk to her... please, papi... talk to her... she's the most understanding and compassionate lady I know... she's there for you... even now... she's there for you."

"I know, papá, I know... I try, I really do... but I just seem to hit dead ends and roadblocks... I get so far and smash into brick wall, after brick wall... and that's that... and it would seem my only way out, is to pick a fight... it's always been that way."

"Yeah, I know... but you've already broken your relationship up... all you're doing now is destroying everything... it's like you've smashed it all to pieces, and now you're setting fire to it, constantly adding gas to the flames... you have to stop this... not just for you... but for Kristie... Kristie, more than anybody... she's the love of your life... she's the best thing that's ever happened to you... and to see you like this... to see you both like this... it's torture to me... it kills me... it's killing all of us... we just want to see you back together... we want you at the parties and get-togethers... we hate seeing you alone... please... papi, please do something about this."

"I'm trying... please believe me... I'm trying." Enrique pleads with his father to understand how difficult this is for him.

"Look, papo... I know you're trying, and I get that you suffer over your mom... you always have... and I know the subject is off limits... and I take full responsibility for that... when I look back... I feel that at times it was like, you were the parent... you were the one that was there for me... when I should have been there for you... if I were a better father to you, instead of wallowing in my own sea of self-pity... you would do better at handling things, as far as this is concerned."

"Papá, you were always there for me... please, don't blame yourself... and it wasn't self-pity... it was grief... it still is... you'd just lost your wife... besides, I just wanted to be normal, like the other kids... and not talking about it, made me normal... made me feel normal... you were, and still are, the best father in the world... you more than made up for two parents... I wanted for nothing, especially love... it's not like that, honestly... I just need to man the fuck up."

"Thanks, papo... but I will never accept that... no matter how much you say it... I know what I was like."

"You were suffering... beyond comprehension... it was a terrible time... you did your best... and you *were,* and still are, the best father in the world." Enrique smiles.

"Thanks, papo," José replies, taking a sip of his cafécito. "And you are the best son I could ever ask for... the very best... and I'm so proud of you."

"Thanks, dad." Enrique smiles shily; he's never very good at compliments.

They sit quietly for a few moments, before José tries to put an idea he has just had into words; he's been wracking his brains to find a way to help his son, and finally, he's thought of something that might work.

"Uh... I mean... I don't know how you would feel about it... but... I could help... like, would I be able to help in some way?" José treads very carefully as he knows that his son is super private when it comes to his emotions, and especially when it comes to Kristie. The fact that he's talking to him so openly right now is such a privilege, and he's not taking it lightly.

"Help? Help, how?" Enrique asks.

"Well, would it help if perhaps I spoke to Krissy... like explained things for you... I don't know... like, I know it's your business, your emotions... but I hate to see you both like this... I hate to see you apart...

you're both suffering so much, and all I want to do is help... help get you two back together... just like you were always meant to be."

"I don't know, dad," Enrique says, letting out a long, slow breath.

"I know... it might be a bit weird... but I could explain things to her... maybe you will find it easier to talk to me... as we went through it together... I don't know... like, I know we know how we both feel... we have a kind of unspoken understanding when it comes to our grief... but, maybe you would be able to open up to me a little more... and I could explain it to her... or we could sit down together... talk over coffee." José shakes his head, not knowing if he's making any sense. "I know it sounds strange... I just want to help, that's all."

"I know, dad... but I couldn't," Enrique replies with gratitude. "Thank you for the offer, but I have to do this by myself... I *have* to... it wouldn't be right coming from anybody else... and I love you for suggesting it and wanting to help... but having you there... would only add to my pressure... not because you pressure me in any way... I just find it that difficult to talk about... having another person there would only exacerbate my fear."

"OK... I understand... it was just a thought, that's all... I would do anything to see you back together... to help."

"I know you would… and so would I… but I can't seem to quite get there."

"You will."

They go quiet again for a few moments, and Enrique looks up at the picture on the wall in front of him; it's a picture of his mom. He studies the black and white portrait of this most beautiful lady, a lady he was so fortunate to spend the first six years of his life with… a lady he was privileged enough to call his mom. He misses her so much, and he knows she would never want any of this for him… he knows that in his heart.

Gina looks so beautiful and elegant as she smiles at the camera, with her long, black, wavy hair cascading over her bare shoulders and over her black strapless dress. She looks so happy; her eyes are bright and sparkling with joy.

José catches his son, looking at the picture, lost in thought. "She was so beautiful." He says.

"She sure was."

"I took that photo just after my life really got started… when she told me she was pregnant with you." José shakes his head with a smile, and brown eyes full of tears. "Christ, we were so happy… ecstatic."

Enrique has heard this story so many times before, but he never gets tired of hearing it.

"The day I met her... my whole world changed... I couldn't get enough of being around her... being in her company." José says. "When I went to The Bounty... which was every weekend, I would always ask for your mom to be the waitress for our table," he says as he remembers the time fondly. "I just loved spending time with her, even if it was just a couple of seconds." His handsome face lights up with a smile, before saying. "But she made me work so hard for a date... but finally she gave in to the José Cruz charm." His smile widens at the memory. "It was a crazy time... all the wait staff would fight over celebrities and the like... people would drop two to three grand on a tip... we'd all drink so much DP we'd run the house dry." He chuckles. "It was madness." He shakes his head. "Such excess."

"That was the 80s!" Enrique says in an upbeat fashion.

"It sure was."

"One of the best eras yet."

"I agree, although I would change some things about it."

"What like?" Enrique asks with confusion. Then something dawns on him. "The world you were in?"

"Yeah, that... but the violence... the violence was out of control... it was a tough time for the city... it's what made Miami what she is today... and she survived it... but a lot of people didn't." Tears fill his eyes. "Miami is a beautiful city... but she has scars... scars that run deep... just like all of us."

"I know, papá... I know." Enrique says, putting his hand on his father's shoulder; he knows what his dad is talking about when he says about scars and surviving pain... he also knows that he's talking about his mom, Gina. "We miss her, huh?" He says sweetly.

"Every second of every day, papito," José says. "And it only gets harder."

"I know," Enrique says in agreement. "I know."

"Papi, please." José pleads. "Don't let this get in the way of you living your life... your mamá would never want this for you... a life of pain and grief... please... let go of it... let go of the pain... the heartache... it will never serve you... if you don't take charge of it now... it will take over the rest of your life... please, papi... live your life... let it go... release the pain. To get to the joy... you have to release the pain... Krissy is your joy... your love...

your life... release the pain... so you can have the joy that is Kristie."

Enrique nods, looking at his father with tears in his eyes, before shifting his blue eyes back to the photo of his mom. As he looks up at her smiling back at him, he begs her to guide him... to help him find a way to do exactly what his father has just advised him to do.

Chapter 16
Monday, May 7th, 2018

Enrique's exhausted as he's spent all night last night and today obsessing about Kristie going out on Saturday night and worrying that someone else will snap her up. When he found out that she went out on the town last night, as he sat on the balcony, the devil was working his magic, and he couldn't see through the fog... the mist of rage that was bubbling inside of him. Jealousy is a sick emotion at the best of times; of course, he's felt it before, but only on a level that would be considered as healthy... but this is far from healthy... this is toxic... this is dangerous, destructive, and harmful to him, and he can't seem to control it. Of course, he hasn't said anything to Kristie about this, as he knows how ridiculous he's being, but he sure as hell has been thinking and feeling it, and the more time he spends dwelling on this, the bigger the monster grows.

What he feels is not only extreme jealousy, but extreme frustration, too; frustration at himself for not dealing with things. He knows what he needs to do to remedy all of this, but he just can't seem to get a grip.

A few minutes ago, during a fairly positive conversation, Kristie told him on the phone that she would love nothing more than for them to get back together again, but she can't go through any of that again; she loves him, but he needs to do something about his grief issues. In that moment, he didn't appreciate where the conversation was heading... so he picked a fight with her instead of talking to her about what was really wrong. Inside, he was telling himself that this was the wrong thing to do, but he kept on doing it for reasons he did not know.

Consumed with blistering jealousy, he hung up the phone and didn't call her back... and he won't! He's angry... angry at himself, and for reasons that illude him, he's angry at her. He knows she's done nothing wrong, but he can't seem to help himself; it's just the way he feels.

He's really going through so many different emotions and has been since the turn of the year, and he really wishes things would let up because, quite frankly, he's had enough of this shit! He would do anything to have a clear mind right now... he would do anything for some peace and tranquility, but it doesn't seem to be what the universe has planned for him, and he's had it with living this way!

Yes, he misses his mom, he misses her like crazy, but his father is right, she would never want him to live this way, she would want him to be happy, and being with Kristie is what makes him happy. He needs to find a way to get through this, or he really is going to lose the best thing that's ever happened to him, if he hasn't done already.

At the moment, he and Kristie might be apart and living separately, but as long as they have contact, he feels that there's a chance that they could reconcile, but if he keeps acting the way he has with her tonight, he knows it's the quickest way to losing her for good... again, his father is right about that too. This type of behavior is what drove her to leave in the first place; but what is he to do? It's the most frustrating thing in the world to know what you need to do to fix a problem, but for it to be so impossible, you can't do it.

* * *

Tuesday, May 8th, 2018

Once again, Kristie comes home to her empty apartment and puts Aretha Franklin on over the sound system while she gets ready for bed after a late finish. She thinks about the situation with her and Enrique; this morning, he called her to apologize once again, she knows this cycle is not good for either of them, but she knows his lashing out is a by-product of his frustration of not being able to do what he knows he needs to do.

She worries so much about his drinking, she keeps hearing all kinds of things about him being out of control, and today, she has just been told something else. In fairness, she has never seen him like this since she left or spoken to him when this supposedly happens, so she's not sure if it is just hearsay or people stirring the pot.

She and Enrique have always been super private about their lives, even though they are known publicly to a certain extent due to Enrique's status, and now hers, plus their presence at galas and the like. Even with all that said, for the most part, they can live their lives under the radar, which they're glad about, but they themselves also help the situation immensely by not feeding into the rumor mill... but sadly, right now, it would appear that Enrique might not be so self-aware when he's been out recently.

She has already mentioned it to him while trying to keep her distance and not be overbearing with it, but he denies it every time. "They're exaggerating." He told her. "You have to understand that this is Miami, and people make things up all the time." He said another time. "But I worry it must be coming from somewhere." She replied. To which he just said that there's nothing to worry about. "It's just not true." He confirmed.

Not knowing what to do with the information she has been told today, she decides to send him a quick text to see how he is. He texts back.

If you're free for
a chat, then so am I.
xxxxx

Kristie finds Enrique's number in her cell and calls him.

"Hey, babe," Enrique says cheerfully, as he answers the phone to Kristie.

"Hey." Kristie replies just as sweetly; she takes comfort in hearing his voice, she misses him so much, and hearing that he sounds relatively upbeat makes her feel a whole lot better after what she's been hearing about him hitting the bottle hard at weekends. She wondered if she would see him out this weekend, but she didn't; on the very few occasions she has been out, she has never seen Enrique, which might be a good thing if these rumors are true.

"How was your day?" He asks.

"It was good, thanks... super busy... I felt better once we'd cleared the air."

"I'm so sorry, darling... I shouldn't have snapped at you that way."

"It's OK... it's a lot... emotions are running high."

"It's no excuse, though."

"It's not an excuse, babe... it's a reason." She says softly... always the voice of reason; she understands Enrique better than anybody, and when he behaves the way he did last night, it's because he's struggling with his emotions, it has nothing to do with her directly.

"You're always so understanding, baby." He says in Spanish. "You understand me... you see me."

"I do, babe... I always have." She says.

"I know." His voice begins to shake... his heart is breaking. "I miss you." He says before he can stop himself.

Kristie goes quiet; she's trying to process what she's just heard. She knows in her heart that he misses her and that he's been destroyed by all of this, but he doesn't really give a lot away when it comes to his feelings these days.

"I'm sorry... I shouldn't have said that." He says apologetically. "It's not fair on you... I know it's not... but I do... I miss you so goddamn much." He takes a breath. "Oh, God... I've done it again... please, forgive me."

"It's OK, babe... I feel the very same... I'm just surprised, that's all... surprised you said it... I don't know... sometimes I wonder if you actually do."

"Oh, baby, I do... I miss you like crazy... no words can ever describe how much I miss you... not seeing you is complete torture... not being able to hold you... to touch you... to kiss you."

"Your lips on mine." She says with a whisper.

"Yes." His voice is barely audible.

"Feeling you... feeling you on top of me... kissing me... caressing me...."

"Your silky skin on my fingertips... as I feel you... feel every curve... every single delicious curve of your beautiful body...."

"Feeling me... all of me... me, feeling all of you." Kristie's breath hitches, as she says what she feels.

"Oh, God, babe... I would do anything... anything, right now... to be with you... to feel you... to hold you... even just to wrap my arms around you, feel you close to me... to close my eyes, and breathe in your glorious scent... to look into your beautiful brown eyes and tell you how much I love and adore you."

"Oh, Enrique... I would do anything to be with you, too." Kristie replies. "Anything."

"Oh, baby... remember when we used to do this... when I was up in New York or wherever," Enrique says.

"Yes... I would be at home... or at work... we didn't care where we were... we just had to be as intimate as we could, even though we couldn't be together... we had to do the next best thing, until we saw each other again... then we would make love for hours... all night... and if we were off work the next day... we'd make love all day too... it was so beautiful... so special...."

"It was... it always is... making love with you... feeling you... connecting with you the way we do... the way only we can... it's always so beautiful... so erotic... *you* are so erotic... so sensual... so feminine... your beautiful body... so perfect... so sexy... your beautiful eyes... your beautiful face... your lips... your breasts... so sexy... so sensitive... so responsive... so...." He stops himself. He is beyond aroused... so aroused he feels like he's about to explode. He adjusts himself, trying to ease the ache he feels in his groin; he misses Kristie beyond belief, more so now than ever, but this isn't fair... it's not fair on her. He worries that doing something like this with her will confuse things, and he respects her more than anything; he would never want her to feel anything other than positive when it comes to their love life, especially. Yes, he's messed things up in so many ways, but when it comes to this... their love... their intimacy... her giving her body to him, be it over the phone or otherwise, he just can't... he can't do it... it's wrong, and he has to be stronger than this. She's vulnerable, and so is he... and sadly, he has to be the one who saves them from themselves.

"Are you OK, babe?" Kristie asks.

"I'm sorry." He whispers.

"What for?" Kristie sounds confused; she's still caught up in her feelings.

"For this… for letting things get this far… for disrespecting you."

"Disrespecting me?"

"Yes." He says simply.

"How?"

"Because, baby girl… I know how you're feeling right now… I know what I've done to you… how I've screwed things up and hurt you so terribly… doing something like that with you… over the phone, or in any way, to me, is disrespectful. Making love with you has always meant so much to me… it's always so special… it's something that's very sacred… I know we could be a little… ya know… well, let's put it this way… I know I should be going to confession a whole lot of times for the things we got up to." He manages a chuckle as he lightens the mood.

Kristie giggles with him. "I must say… you do have a lot of sins to confess, my hot, sexy Catholic Cuban." She jests. "We both do."

He swallows, trying to contain himself as he hears her call him hers, for the first time in way too long. "I will always be yours, baby." He whispers.

"Then be mine." She whispers back, as tears fill her eyes.

"I am... forever." He whispers back.

"I'm forever yours."

"Oh, baby," Enrique replies, his words are barely recognizable.

"What on earth went so wrong." Kristie bursts into tears, she can't control her emotions. She misses this man so much and wants him back in her life more than anything in the world. "It was like a dream come true... we were going to get married." Kristie cries.

"Please, don't cry, baby," Enrique says. "I will do anything for you... anything."

"And I will do anything for you, Enrique." Kristie sobs. "But we can't... we can't go back to that."

"But we won't... we will make it different this time." He promises. And as he says his words, he means them, he really does... but at the same time, he knows that he can't open up about his grief... he wants to, but something inside of him is stopping him... it's like he has some kind of blockage that is refusing to budge, and it's killing him inside. "I want to... but it just won't happen," Enrique says, with devastation in his voice. "I don't know why... but it just won't... I'm trying... I'm trying so hard...

and it's killing me… I'm dying inside, Krissy… literally dying."

Kristie cries some more. "Oh, Enrique."

"Please, baby… I really want to find a way… but I don't know where to start… I… I just don't know what to do… which way to turn."

"I love you so much." She whispers.

"And I love you so much too, baby… more than you will ever know… I just don't know what I'm supposed to do with this whole… uh… situation… it's hell on earth."

"I know it is." She says, wiping her tears. "I hate it."

"Me too, baby… me too." He says. "I'm so sorry… I'm so sorry for everything… for it all… I really thought I could do it… I thought I could find a way… but it's just so impossible… and it's not fair on you to have to put up with my shit and the way I kept treating you… the way I *have* been treating you… being OK one minute, and the next, flying off the handle… you deserve better… way better."

"But I want you… I want us."

"I do, too… more than anything… but it's like this part of me is locked away… in a box… and I can't find the key… I can't find a way to unlock that part of me… and until I do… I'm going to always have this side of me... I'm always going to slip into darkness, or whatever you want to call it... I'm always going to fall back into that way because I haven't fixed the root of the problem... I might be messed up... but I'm sane enough and aware enough to know that... and you don't need that in your life... it breaks my heart into a trillion pieces, but I can't keep doing that to you... I love you more than anything... you're my person... my world... I have to fix this somehow."

Kristie nods; he's right... as painful as it is... he's right... and for the first time, it actually feels like he's starting to figure things out, or at least making a start on figuring things out; this gives her hope.

"Baby?" Enrique says.

"Yes... yes... I'm still here." She pauses before continuing. "Thank you." She says.

"What for?" He replies, sounding extremely confused. "What on earth have you got to thank me for? You have nothing to thank me for, baby."

"For being you."

"OK. Now, you really do have me confused."

"Because of what you just did." She says sweetly. "You were right... I was caught up in the moment... and as much as I love doing that with you... you know how much I love doing that with you... I love making love to you in any way... but you were right... I'm not in the right frame of mind for that right now.... and you know how I feel about intimacy... it's been difficult for me at times... and the fact that you put my feelings ahead of your own... something you have always done... especially when it comes to making love... it means the world to me... I've always known that you're a true gentleman... even when things got bad... I have always known this... and I want you to know that I appreciate you and how much you respect me... respect my feelings."

"Always, baby." He says. "I know I've been terrible to you... the way I've treated you... but when it comes to our intimacy... when it comes to loving you... I could never cross any line... ever... it's a non-negotiable... I know I've stupidly crossed many lines I should never have crossed... and I know I've hurt you in so many ways... which I regret tremendously... if I could go back in time and change it all, I would... but I could never do anything to hurt you in that way... or do something that will make you feel regretful about it afterward... I would never forgive myself."

"I know, babe... and that's why I wanted to say thank you... it's hard... it's so difficult right now... all I want is you... all I want is you, in every way... but I know that's not possible... but at least we can be friends... at least we can talk on the phone."

"Exactly." This kills Enrique. Things shouldn't be this way between them, Kristie should be at home with him; but there's no other option right now.

They both say their goodbyes and tell each other that they love each other, before heading to bed for yet another restless night's sleep alone.

As Enrique pulls back the sheets, his eyes home in on the picture Kristie gifted him on their first Valentine's Day together... a picture of the two of them together on the night they finally met... a picture he hasn't had the courage to move. Just like every time he finds himself looking at this photo, since they've been apart, his heart breaks when he sees how happy they were... how in love they so obviously were from the very first moment they met... why can't they go back to that time... a time when things were so simple... so easy.

As he lays in bed alone, all of a sudden, a thought enters his mind... just go to therapy... work on this shit... make it better... just go to therapy... it's that simple.

He reaches for his cell with urgency and unlocks the screen. He's going to do it... he's going to find a therapist and call them first thing tomorrow... his first step to fixing himself, as well as this mess he's caused... he's going to do it... before he can even think about it a second longer, he's going to do it!

Turning down the brightness on his cell, as it's super bright with the lights off, he finds the internet icon and selects it. He then taps on the search bar, and the keyboard appears on the screen… as his thumb hovers over the letter *T* on the keyboard, his hands begin to shake. He feels nauseous, and his heart begins to race to the point where he feels like it's going to jump out of his chest. Fuck!!! I can't… I can't! I can't fucking do this!

He knows in his heart that Kristie is right about this… she has been all along, and he also knows that he doesn't want to burden her with his shit… so, therapy is the best answer… by going to see someone professional, they will help him find the tools to help him deal with his grief, and figure out a way of talking to Kristie about this… it's the best thing he can do for himself, but more importantly, for Kristie and their relationship.

With his left hand falling back down on the bed, as he holds his cell, he raises his right forearm to his head and rests it across his eyes, feeling sick to the stomach once again. He's had enough of this shit. Why can't he just do this? Why the fuck can't he just make that call… take the first step to helping himself… to helping him fix things with Kristie? He wants this more than anything in the world… all he wants is him and Kristie living happily ever after, enjoying life the way they used to… but the problem is, he knows what going to therapy will mean, and he knows exactly what he will have to do when he goes there... he will have to face his demons... he will have to feel the excruciating agony he felt back when he was six years old... the agony that made him cry all the time, and feel physically sick... he can't do it... he can't put himself through that again, because he's petrified that he will never feel anything but that devastation, and pain ever again.

What if going to therapy is like opening a can of worms... what if when he does actually talk about it, he will never be the same again... he won't be able to hide from it at all, and will live in a state of perpetual misery? But isn't that what you're living right now? A voice whispers in his head. You're the most miserable you have ever been... you're not happy... you're more depressed and lower than you've ever been... just rip the Band-Aid off... rip open the wound, and scoop out the poison... then heal... heal with the love of Kristie.

But he can't. He just can't do it.

Chapter 17
Thursday, May 10th, 2018

Enrique is super frustrated with himself, yet again. He came so close to doing what he knows he needs to do but still couldn't make it. He's so angry with himself, too, so angry that he finds himself drinking even more this week. When he speaks to Kristie, he acts like everything's OK, but it's really not. But he acts this way as he doesn't want to burden her any more than he already has done.

Right now, he is at la ventanita at La Caretta restaurant in Little Havana, talking in Spanish to some old Cuban guys who are friends of his late grandparents, on his father's side. They talk about their views on the new president, who has recently been sworn in, plus various other issues with the island, like the hospital situation, food, and repression, plus general life in Cuba.

"You know, papito." One of the men says, as he sips his cafécito. "We're so grateful to be living here... in this amazing country... where we're free... I will never take it for granted... not ever... but God, do I miss the island... so, so much... there's nowhere like Cuba... nowhere on earth."

"Well, hopefully, one day, I will get to experience it," Enrique says. "But you're right... we're so lucky to be living this life." He says, puffing on a cigar, then ordering some more coffee as he stands talking to the men. "I will never take it for granted."

"I know, papo… you get it." Another man says. "You appreciate this life… like your girlfriend… Kristie…."

Enrique nods, taking a long draw from his cigar as he sits at the counter. He doesn't have the heart to tell the man that they are no longer together.

"What she does for the gay people." The man says.

"Incredible," Enrique says… he's so proud of her. He feels terrible talking about her and all her achievements like they're still together, when they're not… it's almost like nothing's changed… but everything's changed at the same time, and it's heartbreaking for him. "She's incredible… she works so hard to help the community… and she wants to do more… amongst other things."

"Yes, it is incredible… I mean, in my day… it was always kept under wraps… but now, everybody is so open… so out there… and good for them… I applaud it… but back home… it's still illegal… you get put in jail for being gay… it's insane… crazy… like who are the government to tell you who you can love… who you can be?"

"Exactly." Enrique agrees. "It's a disgrace… and it needs to change."

"It will… it has to, papito." The other man says. "But not with this new guy… he might make minor changes… but the regime needs to go, for any real change."

"I know… and it can't come a moment too soon." Enrique agrees. "Like, remember when Castro died, and everybody was outside Versailles, celebrating, with los cacerolazos, honking their horns and everything?" He smiles.

"Yeah… I remember… we all do… we were all there… that day was a good day." One of the men says. "But things are still very much the same."

"I know… but we have hope… we always have hope… hope for freedom for our country… freedom for our people…."

"Exactly, papi… and it will come… it will come… I just hope I live to see it… I mean, I'm 86 now."

"You'll see it… you're still a young spring chicken!" Enrique says with a cheery smile, although he feels anything but cheerful right now.

"Flattery will get you everywhere, papito." The man says. "Everywhere!"

They all laugh together and chat some more over another cafécito.

On the way home in the car, Enrique's listening to the radio, and "Baby I Need Your Loving" by Four Tops comes on. He finds himself singing to the words, forgetting what it's about for a second, he loves this song; he and Kristie used to listen to Motown a lot... he begins to feel happy for a moment, then all of a sudden, the words begin to resonate with him, and he feels the agony in his heart once again. His happy memory of Kristie and him, turns to devastation once more.

He turns off the radio and drives the rest of the journey in silence.

He pulls up at the valet and thanks Jorge for taking the white Rolls Royce to the parking lot. He then heads up to the penthouse and makes himself some more coffee.

Just as he selects his John Newman playlist on his phone, links it to the sound system in the penthouse, and presses play, his cell rings. It's García.

"Hey, buddy boy... coming out tonight?" He asks, full of Cuban cheer.

It's obvious García is drunk already. Enrique checks his watch, the platinum blue-faced Rolex that Kristie gifted him for his birthday last year. "Papo... it's 4 o'clock on a Thursday, and you're fucked already?" Enrique says, playfully admonishing his friend.

"Yeah, well… I took the day off… Rico finished at lunchtime… so we decided to come to this amazing pool party down on South Beach… I'm telling you, papo… there are some hot chicks here today… wearing next to nothing… ya know… it's nice." He says in a drunken, yet matter-of-fact tone. "It's been a good day, papá… we caught some rays… had some fucking awesome mojitos… and… well… there's lots of fun to be had… let me tell you… you should get your ass down here and join in the fun… put a smile on that handsome face of yours."

"Yeah… not tonight, papo… I've got a shit ton of work to do… I got a deadline."

"Such a fucking bore," García says playfully.

"Nothing boring about me, papo… just got work to do… thought that you might do the same… but it would seem you have better things to do on this weekday afternoon, like get fucked in more ways than one."

"Bro… there's always time for that," García says.

"Come on, pretty boy… get your ass down here!" Sánchez shouts down the phone.

García puts Enrique on loudspeaker.

"I've got too much work to do… some of us have a company to run… ya know… that thing called work... like most people, on a Thursday afternoon," Enrique says, sounding all parental; for once, he's actually being sensible.

"Ugh, so boring... you wanna watch out, pretty boy... you'll get old before your time, if you're not careful," Sánchez says jokingly.

"Never gonna happen," Enrique says with certainty. "Just have responsibilities... just like you."

"Oh yeah... who was the one telling you to slow down the other week... as you've been drinking so much of your favorite Havana Club, lately... ya know... the one that they only produce one thousand bottles a year... it's like you're trying to drink them all... keeping them all to yourself."

"Yeah, exactly... not boring," Enrique says, sounding all serious... but it's all part of their banter.

"You're still boring... there's pussy everywhere... like literally everywhere I look... and you wanna stay home," Sánchez says, knowing that Enrique wouldn't be interested, but he says it anyway.

"Yes, bro... home is exactly where I will stay tonight... now... can you leave this very boring, old man in peace so he can run his company... now, Papi Chulo... go run... be free... and use a condom... or six." Enrique manages a small chuckle.

"Oh, papi… you know us… we might be wild… but we're not crazy… García's handbag is full of rubbers… oh… and lube." Sánchez, jests.

"I'm going… you two disgust me… now fuck off!" Enrique jokes.

"OK, Abuelo… sleep well… don't forget your hot cocoa before bed," García says.

"And you can fuck off, too," Enrique says.

They all say their goodbyes, and Enrique gets back to his coffee. He fills the white espresso cup to the brim with cafécito and makes his way upstairs to get changed. He's going to put something comfortable on and work well into the night… he has so much to do.

Once upstairs, he takes a sip of his espresso and places the cup down on the nightstand in the bedroom, then heads to the closet and gets changed into some sweats and a t-shirt. He quickly uses the bathroom and makes his way back to the bedroom, using the other bathroom door instead of walking through the closet, like he usually does.

As he reaches for the door handle, he notices Kristie's silk robe on the back of the bathroom door; this stops him in his tracks. He reaches for the sleeve of the robe, and before he can stop himself, he lifts the silk to his nose and inhales; it still smells of her... his beautiful girl and her perfume, Coco Chanel. He closes his eyes as he takes comfort in the glorious scent... if only she were here now... here with him, in his arms... but she's not... she's not here because of him and his crap... his issues... his darkness... and it would appear there's not a damn thing he can do about it... or at least, not a damn thing he's capable of doing, anyway.

He slowly opens his eyes and tries to take comfort in the fact that he's just discovered another item of Kristie's, just like the nightdress he found under the pillow and her shower gel in the bathroom cupboard, plus he found some other items that she has left behind too, including the Fortnum and Mason's tea they brought back from the U.K. on one of their many vacations. As heartbreaking as it is to find these things, he finds it somewhat comforting to still have some of her things around. He knows he should really package them up and send them to her, but he can't face it.

Feeling derailed once more, he opens the door to the bathroom, heads into the bedroom, picks up his cafécito, and makes his way downstairs to his office, where he will work until the early hours.

* * *

At approximately 2am, he decides to take a break and makes his way to the kitchen to get some more coffee, then he heads out to the balcony for some air and to give his eyes a break from the computer screen; he should be done in an hour or two, then he will go to bed... hopefully he will get some sleep tonight... but he doesn't hold out much hope.

With his John Newman playlist shuffling to the ballad version of "Out of My Head," he listens to the words, letting them wash over him as he takes stock of his devastating situation.

He thinks back to his friend's phone call earlier... they're right... he has been drinking a lot of rum lately... and if he's honest, they're probably the only people that can get away with calling him out on his shit, at the moment... probably because they're in absolutely no position to do so. But they're right... he has been drinking way too much... and as much as he keeps telling himself that he will slow down... he never seems to... another plan he can't seem to execute.

He knows he's been sedating his pain... a pain caused by losing the love of his life... his one and only... his beautiful, beautiful brunette, that he fell in love with the very moment he laid eyes on her... he misses everything about her... everything... he misses her love... the look she gives him... a look that tells him everything... there's no need for words... he misses her touch... the glorious sensation of her lips on his... the feeling of her in his arms... her voice... her voice telling him how much she loves him... he misses laying out here, on this very balcony, watching the boats out on the bay, as they listen to music and talk… he misses the feeling of her body against his… their love for each other… their love that is so powerful and passionate… to the point where they were so hungry for each other, it was like they were starved… their need for each other was so primal, and carnal… so intense and mind-blowing… yet also, so pure and gentle… so tender and sweet… so beautiful.

His heart is broken… his soul is crushed… it's like someone has turned the lights off… he's in complete darkness… in complete darkness, because he can't seem to get it together… he can't do what needs to be done… he can't open up to her… just like he told her… it's like everything's locked inside of him, and he can't find the key. He's carrying so much anger… so much frustration… anger and frustration at himself, and he knows he keeps taking it out on Kristie, and it's not her fault at all… none of this is… as all she did was fall in love with him… all she did was love him and treat him with the utmost kindness and respect.

With his head spinning in about a thousand different directions, he asks himself, why the fuck, do I have to keep fucking it, the fuck up? What the fuck is wrong with me? Call her, and tell her everything… talk to her… but he just can't seem to get the words out… well, first and foremost… he can't even find the words, as he has no way of explaining how he feels… he's incapable…

incapable of expressing himself and the fucked-up mess inside of him... the fucked-up mess, that is completely invisible from the outside... everybody thinks Enrique Cruz has everything under control... everything is exactly how it should be... every detail is taken care of... every single part of his life is in order with great precision... well, the fact of the matter is, he isn't in control of shit, and he's angry, frustrated, and also embarrassed at himself for being such a mess, that he's lost the only person he's ever loved... the person that gave him everything and more... the only person he's given his heart to... Kristie Carrington.

As he sits, sipping his coffee, looking out over the bay of darkness, the bay of darkness that's mirroring his feelings and mood, he can feel his mom watching over him. He looks up to the dark, starry sky with tear-filled eyes... he knows that she disapproves of his behavior... he knows that she will be disappointed in him for the way he's behaved. Not only does he feel like he's let Kristie down, but he's let his mom down, too. He can't help but feel like she's trying to guide him, but he's so lost... he has no clue how to follow her lead... he has no clue what to do... he feels like he's in freefall, and all he can do is ride it out... and put his trust in God... put his trust in his beloved mom, to help guide him back into the light... guide him back to himself... but most of all... guide him back to Kristie.

Chapter 18
Friday, May 11th, 2018

Kristie is at work and is looking through her schedule. Her mom has invited her over for dinner, and she's figuring out which evenings she will be working late due to some extra appointments for a couple of wedding glam consultations.

As she looks through her diary, she flicks back to the previous week and notices that her period is late. With concern etched across her face, she flicks through to the previous month; she's sure she's just a little late due to all the stress she's been under. As she checks to see if she's got the dates mixed up, she tells herself that if it's not the stress, perhaps she's worked it out wrong and wrote in the wrong date, that she should be expecting her period this month.

Kristie is on the pill, but she likes to keep track of her periods as she used to have such terrible trouble with them, so she still likes to keep an eye on them and by doing this, she writes in when she should expect her period and when she actually had it, of course, this is in code, so nobody will know what it is, if by any chance anybody sees her diary open.

As she looks through the previous month, her heart stops; she's missed her period the previous month, too. She forces herself to take a deep breath, trying to calm herself down as she's beginning to shake. No... no, I can't be... no! She takes another deep breath. She's in turmoil right now... how can it be?

Then, she appeases herself by telling herself that she's been through hell and it's completely normal to miss periods during times of stress... plus there's even a chance that she could have got so side-tracked that she actually had the periods she thinks she missed, and forgot to write them down. It will be OK. Things will work themselves out, just give it time.

Pushing her concerns aside, she notices the time and reapplies her lipstick, then checks her hair and make-up in the mirror, readying herself for her next client. She will text her mom later when she has more time to check through things and she's a little calmer.

She stands and takes another deep breath, telling herself that everything is going to be OK, before making her way out of her office to greet her next client.

* * *

Later that evening

Kristie is on the phone with Enrique as she walks through the door of her apartment; she's just finished a long day, and she's ready for a hot bath, then straight to bed. She hasn't and won't discuss anything about what happened while she was checking her schedule earlier on today; she's sure it's just stress, and the last thing she wants to do is worry Enrique with something that he doesn't need to be worried about.

"Ya know, I was thinking earlier today about how much I miss your family," Kristie says to Enrique with sadness.

"Yeah?" He replies softly; this kills him inside because he knows that this is all his fault.

"Yeah, like at the weekend, I drove past the restaurant, and... I dunno... it's like, I nearly stopped by for a coffee... out of habit, I guess... I'm just so used to being able to do that... but now I feel... I dunno... like, strange, I guess."

"Baby, my grandparents... the whole family would love to see you... they always will... they love you... please don't feel like that." Enrique says sweetly.

"Aww, thanks for saying that, babe... it just feels awkward now, ya know... now we're not...."

"I know, baby... but please... my grandparents miss you... I know they do... my dad... everybody misses you." He wants to tell her that he misses her desperately, to the point where sometimes he feels like he's going to die, but he refrains; he doesn't want to upset her anymore. "Please." He says. "If you're passing... please stop by... I know they would love it so much."

"I guess I should stop overthinking things and just do it."

"Please, there's no need to give it another thought... I know they would love it... mami, you're still family... you always will be." He manages a small smile. "We're Cuban at the end of the day, baby... family is everything... please, go visit them... they would love it... please don't let my stupidity... my screw-ups, stop you from seeing people you love." He says with deep meaning... and he really does mean it, more than anything.

Once they end the call, he sits up on the pool deck with a cigar and some rum, beating himself up about the complete mess he has made of everything. His actions... his issues have caused a domino effect that has made such a difference to so many people's lives, not just his and Kristie's... he really has fucked up!

The fact that he couldn't open up to Kristie and destroyed their relationship, has had a knock-on effect and has caused such a negative impact on so many people, like his beloved grandparents, his father, and so on. Kristie was, and still is, very much loved by his entire family... they all adore her, and to think that the way he's acted... the fact he ruined their relationship, has now left Kristie feeling too awkward to visit the people she used to visit all the time, with or without him, without giving it a second thought... this absolutely breaks his heart.

He takes a sip of his rum, then puffs on his cigar as he thinks about the way things used to be. Both families hit it off straight away, and it was such joy to be part of such an amazing dynamic; everybody got on so well, even their friends got on like a house on fire! He's basically torn apart their two families, plus their friends, and he feels like absolute shit about it; he's ashamed of himself for what he has done, especially to Kristie, but to everyone else, too. I have to fix this! I have to do something! He then circles back to the same old conclusion and drives himself deeper into a state of depression, anxiety, and frustration... how much longer can he live this way?

* * *

The following day

Enrique is sitting in his office in the company building, staring at his iMac computer, but he can't see anything that's on the screen in front of him; he's lost in deep thought. During this rare moment, work is the last thing on his mind... he's reliving the conversation he had with Kristie last night about their families and how he felt afterward. With Mother's Day looming, he can't help but think how important family is.

He misses Kristie like crazy, just like always, but right now, he can't help but think about how much he misses her parents, too; they took him in like their own and loved him so much, just like he loves them... they enriched his life in so many ways.

Of course, he misses Viv, she is such a wonderful lady and so kind-hearted and sweet, but he misses seeing Jon a lot, too. He misses their incredible relationship... and going out with him on the boat, but he's pretty sure Kristie's father wouldn't want to see him right now or any time soon.

As he stares blankly at his computer screen, he remembers an occasion when he arrived at José's house, ready to meet Jon and the boys for a day out fishing; they all got along so well, and had such a great bond, including Jon and José.

He remembers opening the door to his father's Star Island mansion, and all he could hear was The Beatles blasting through the entire Mediterranean-style estate; José was playing it on vinyl.

"Wow, papá... this takes me back!" Enrique shouted over the loud music as he found his father in the kitchen, singing the legendary outro to "Hey Jude."

"You know us Cubanos, papo." He smiles as he pours them some of the espresso he's just made. "Somebody tells us we can't do something... we'll find a way. That son of a bitch Castro tells us we can't listen to The Beatles... we all pass around pirate tapes of The Beatles. Suddenly, we all love The Beatles... even if we've never listened to them before." He laughed. "And one of the earliest memories I have of my father... your grandfather... is listening to The Beatles on his pirate tapes he brought here from Cuba."

"I know... I remember you telling me over the years." Enrique said. "I love it... fuck Castro and his shit!" He said, as he took the cafécito his father was handing him.

"I couldn't agree more," José said as they walked through the great room, with The Beatles still playing. "The only person who could tell me not to do something was your mamá, and I did everything she told me... well, aside from the occasional late night home... but apart from that... I always listened to your mom." He raised his eyebrows with a smile. "And I was right to... she was always right!" He chuckled.

"Well, of course." Enrique chuckled back. "She always was... she had the most incredible sixth sense about her, too."

"She sure did," José said as he opened the patio door, standing aside for Enrique to walk through first.

"Thank you," Enrique said as he stepped out into the humid morning air. He knew exactly what his father was talking about. He was talking about his mom asking him to leave his less-than-legit lifestyle behind him back in the 80s, before they got married; a lifestyle she had no part of but knew he was involved in, and she never liked it. It was never spoken about; José would just tell her he was at work and gave her no other details... and she never asked any questions.

It was OK at first when they were dating; he charmed her for ages... he would literally do anything to gain her attention and impress her before she finally gave in to a date with him, then she fell in love with him quickly. But when she found out she was pregnant with Enrique, she gave him an ultimatum: us or the lifestyle... and José chose them, and Enrique is so happy about it.

He's super proud that his father managed to get out of the underworld back in the 80s before it was too late. Enrique knows how addictive that kind of money would have been to somebody like a young José, coming from the wrong side of the tracks... he also knows that power is the biggest addiction you can ever get hooked on, and things could have very easily gone down a very dark path.

He's so glad José got out before he caught any charges or, even worse, got killed. In that world, there are usually only two ways out: either jail or death, but thankfully, José escaped both. One thing's for sure: it's definitely not a world Enrique would ever get involved in, but he understands how hard things were back then. He's just glad his mom took charge of the situation and gave his father that ultimatum. José's life took a completely different direction when he founded Cruz Construction, plus a ton of other businesses and charities; thank God! Enrique thanks God every day that his parents did the right thing, not just by him, but by themselves, it would have been very easy to have kept it all going, he's very well aware of that. He's so grateful to them both for giving him the opportunities he's had in life and is so blessed because of them; plus, he worships his father, and they have the best relationship.

They headed out to the terrace and took a seat while they waited for the rest of the guys to arrive for their day out fishing.

On the boat, José played Gloria Estefan's "Anything for You" album, as the men fish and chat about anything and everything.

"Wow, I love Gloria Estefan and The Miami Sound Machine," Jon said.

"They're amazing, aren't they?" José said.

"Yes… fantastic! Viv and I went to see them in concert way back in the 80s… '89, I think," Jon said.

"Oh my god, really? The Homecoming Tour?"

"Yes."

"Wow, what a small world," José replied with sweet surprise. "Gina and I went to the very same concert. How crazy is that? It was a brilliant night... the best." He shakes his head with a smile. "Christ, those were the days... Miami was a very different place back then... the best... yet the worst at the same time."

"I agree," Jon said. "We don't want those days back ever again... but there were some fantastic times... the 80s were some of the best years."

"They sure were," José said with sadness.

As Enrique remembers this moment, not only does he find it crazy that both his and Kristie's parents were at the same concert back in the 80s, but he also recalls how he could see his father struggling; he knows that his father misses Gina so desperately, just like he does, and just talking about that concert and remembering the night they had, pulled at his heart, bringing tears to his eyes.

He remembers seeing Jon check in on José, as he could see a shift in his mood. As he watched the two men together, Enrique felt so good that they had the bond that they did... it was so nice to see. When he talked to his father about this, José said that he was thankful for his black wayfarers concealing his emotions. He remembers looking away and out to the ocean, begging for a change of subject to come to his mind quickly. Thankfully, Leon caught a huge fish, and all the men rushed over to him to cheer him on as he reeled it in.

They had so many incredible times together as a family, and he misses those times so much, and it kills him to think that he's lost that too.

Chapter 19
Sunday, May 13th, 2018
Mother's Day

After speaking to Enrique this morning to see if he's OK, due to the significance of today, Kristie meets Lisa for a coffee this morning, then she will meet her mom at lunch and spend the rest of the day with her.

Still ignoring the fact that her period is late, although she knows that if this carries on, she'll need to address it one way or another, she mentions to Lisa that she's been so tired lately and feels a bit out of sorts.

"You're not coming down with something?" Lisa asks, looking all pretty in a light blue floaty mini dress and silver sandals, with her platinum blonde hair tied up in a high pony.

"No... I don't think so... I hope not... I don't have time to be sick." Kristie replies. "My period's late, so it's probably to do with that." She says flippantly, like she's not worried about it at all.

"Your period's late?" Lisa repeats her friend's words at a slow pace. "Krissy, your period's never late... you're the most regular person I know... you're not...."

"No," Kristie says quickly, cutting her friend off before she can say anymore.

"You done a test?" Lisa asks, with raised eyebrows; judging by Kristie's attitude to the situation, she's pretty sure she knows the answer already.

"No," Kristie replies, as she takes a sip of her coffee.

"Why not?" Lisa asks.

"Because I know I don't need to," Kristie says, so sure of what she's saying. "There's been a lot of stress lately, and it's just my body reacting to that... I just need to take better care of myself, that's all... it's been a lot."

"It has been, babe... but come on... this isn't like you, and you've been under stress before... and never had any issues then... and you say you're super tired," Lisa says.

"Babe, I'm tired because I never sleep, and I've been working like crazy... there's no way I could be, anyway." Kristie can't even say the word. "There's no way... I take my pill on time every day and haven't been sick or anything... no medication... nothing... so, there's no way I could be." She says with certainty, and what she's saying is true, there is no reason that she could be pregnant, and she *is* going through the most difficult time of her life, it's so obviously down to that; it will right itself soon enough.

"Well, I think you should do a test, babe... just to be sure... I mean, if you are... this changes everything."

"Lisa, please... I'm not... and it changes nothing." Kristie says, with an air of firmness; Lisa is vocalizing something that Kristie really can't stand to hear right now... she can't even consider the fact that she could be pregnant, it would be the worst time to have a baby right now.

"Krissy, it changes *everything*... Enrique will be over the moon... it will snap him out of his troubles... it will bring you back together again... I know you two are made for each other... and you both know that, too."

"Babe, we can't just get back together because of that... even if it were the case... which it's not. As much as I would love for us to get back together... nothing is changing... Enrique is still Enrique... he's not done anything for me to think otherwise... yes, he's talked about wanting to change, but talking doesn't fix anything... I need to see him *doing* things to help himself... and until that happens, we can never get back together." Tears fill Kristie's eyes as she says what she has to say. "I love him... desperately... and he loves me... but our relationship became so toxic, and it's not good for either of us." Tears fall down her face; she's devastated.

"Aww, babe... he'll find a way... I know he will... I just know." Lisa says with certainty. "Please don't cry." She says, as she looks at her friend with tears in her eyes as she holds her hand across the table.

Kristie nods as she wipes her tears. "Thanks, babe... I just... ugh... I just wish things were different... I wish he would find a way... I wish none of this ever happened, I really do... all I want is for us to be together... I hate not seeing him... I hate being apart from him... it's been so long since we've seen each other... since it happened... and we don't seem to be any further along than we were when I moved out... which makes me wonder if we *are* meant to be together."

"Give it time babe... it's a huge deal... what he's been going through... trying to release years of built-up grief... it will take time for him to finally face things... and when he does... and when you get back together... which you will... things will be even better than they were in the first place... I just know it, babe... I just do."

"Thanks, babe... it's just so hard, ya know... it's so difficult... and not being able to help him in any way... it just makes things even worse."

"I know, babe... but you'll get there... I just know you will... besides, you have helped him... and you still are, by doing what you're doing... it might not feel like it right now... but you're helping him by having this time apart so he can get a handle on things… it will all work out in the end, I just know it will. He loves you so much… he worships you." She squeezes Kristie's hand and smiles.

Kristie nods and smiles through her tears.

"Now… I'm gonna get us the biggest cake they have… I'll make sure it's the most disgustingly chocolaty one, too… I know how much you love chocolate." She smiles. "And we're gonna eat every single bite." She says, as she stands. "My girl is losing weight… something tells me she's not eating properly, despite my lectures on making sure she doesn't skip meals," Lisa says, with raised eyebrows, looking at her friend, all parental and concerned.

"I try to," Kristie says. "I just don't feel like it."

"Well, you're gonna help me eat this cake for now… and I'm gonna cook for you tomorrow night… as I know we're spending the rest of our days with our moms."

"Aww, you're a good friend, Lis', thank you."

"Don't mention it," Lisa replies. "Gonna make you the finest Asian cuisine you will ever taste."

"And I know it will be, babe," Kristie says, smiling through her tears. "It always has been."

"Aww, you're so kind, sweetheart." Lisa smiles. "Now, let me get us this cake so we can sit and devour every last crumb."

* * *

After a lovely afternoon and evening with her mom and dad, Kristie is now getting ready for bed. Her cell vibrates on the vanity; it's Lisa.

Hope you had
a nice time with
your mom?
xxx

Yes, thanks, babe.
How about you?
xxx

Amazing, thanks.
Don't forget to
do that test, babe.
xxx

Kristie replies.

I won't.
xxx

As she writes the message, she knows she won't do the test, she's just saying it to stop Lisa from asking her to do one. She knows she can't be pregnant, she's followed all the rules, so she does her best to put it all out of her mind. What else is she supposed to do?

Chapter 20
Wednesday, May 16th, 2018

It's gone midnight, and once again, Kristie can't sleep; going to bed alone every night for the past six weeks has been complete torture for her, and it's not getting any easier... only harder. She misses Enrique like crazy... all she wants to do is cuddle up to him and drift off to the calming sound of his heartbeat as she rests on his firm chest, just like she has done so many times in the past when she can't sleep. She's all alone and lonelier than ever... and would do anything to have him here with her.

Deciding to follow the advice everybody seems to give you when it comes to insomnia, she gets out of bed and makes her way through her contemporary apartment toward the floor-to-ceiling sliding glass doors, which lead out to the balcony; perhaps some sea air will help calm her, that combined the sound of the ocean crashing against the shoreline, might be just what she needs to relax her weary mind... her weary mind that has been working overtime over the past few months, and the last six weeks, it's been even worse.

As she looks out to the ocean, she leans on the balcony railings, taking in the view of the platinum moonlight glistening on the water; it's so beautiful... like a sea of glitter. Her long white silk nightdress floats effortlessly in the light breeze as she glances out to the horizon, trying to ease the pain in her heart, a pain so agonizing she sometimes wonders how she gets through each day. She's desperately heartbroken by what's happened between her and Enrique and feels that she will never get over it… he's the only man for her… he's all she wants and needs… and she needs to be in his arms more than anything in the world. To feel his love for her as he holds her close… for him to glide his hand over her hair as he holds her and tells her that everything is going to be OK, and that he loves her, just like he has done so many times before. She hates every minute of being apart from him… all she wants is him… all she wants is *them*.

Being without Enrique, the love of her life is the single most painful thing she has ever endured, and she would do anything to get back together with him. Her heart is broken… *she* is broken, and life hasn't been the same since she left, and right now, in this very moment, she regrets that day… as much as she knows it was the right thing to do, she wishes she would have stayed and tried harder… perhaps things would have been different… perhaps they could have fixed things sooner, if she had stayed?

She shakes her head at her thoughts. She knows that she had to leave… even if her heart is telling her otherwise… it was the right thing for both of them… she had to draw a line somewhere… and she can see glimmers of him starting to see things a little differently over the past couple of weeks, he's been less combative and a little more open to talking. As she thinks of this, hope stirs within her... perhaps Lisa is right... perhaps she has to look at them being separated as a way of her giving him time... as a way of helping him... a way of giving him the space he needs to finally face what he needs to, alone... privately... in his own time? Maybe that's what he needs... maybe that's what they both need? But one thing she knows for sure is... Enrique has to see this for himself... no matter how much she tries to help him see... no matter how much she tries to help with this... he has to figure it out alone, as he's the type of person that won't be told... especially when it comes to this.

As she absorbs the calming sound of the ocean waves gently crashing against the shore, she thinks back to the other conversations she's had with Lisa. She still hasn't followed her friend's advice and taken a test, as she feels that she really isn't pregnant... there could be no way... although nothing is one hundred percent, of course... but the chances are so slim, in Kristie's mind, she feels it isn't the case... but then, she thinks about how she would feel if she was.

The truth of the matter is, she doesn't know. She and Enrique have talked about having children, but they both agreed it would be something they would visit way into the future... they have so much they want to do before they venture down that path... thankfully, this was something they both agreed on; getting married is one thing, but children would be a long way off.

She smiles as she remembers a time when she was working one Saturday, and she came home to find Enrique in the pool with Sánchez and García, along with some of his little cousins. They were having an absolute ball... all six of them were splashing around and having fun... all three of those men are so good with kids. She remembers being so surprised at how the party boys, Sánchez and García, were so great with children. She always knew Enrique was, as she'd seen him with his cousins many times before, although he would never admit it to anyone, plus he's so particular about his clothes, and the way he lives... kids make mess... and Enrique hates mess. Kristie manages a little giggle as she thinks about that.

As her mind drifts over the sweet memories of that day, she remembers Hugo, one of his little cousins, saying how much he loves coming to Uncle Enrique's, but it doesn't happen enough. Enrique apologizes and says it's down to his work... he works a lot of hours. "Building those HUGE skyscrapers?!" Hugo says, full of pride and enthusiasm for his uncle's profession. "That's right!" Enrique says, as he tickles Hugo as he holds him in the water. Then García chimes in, saying that it's got nothing to do with work... it's because he spends too much time at the hairdressers and checking himself out in front of the mirror!

Kristie finds herself giggling again, as she remembers one of the many great times they shared together. They had such a wonderful relationship for the most part. Yes, they argued from time to time... but mostly, they got along so well, and their love for each other was, and still is, so deep and so powerful. She misses their connection... she misses everything about him and *them*... she misses the feeling of being in his presence... even if they were in different rooms of the penthouse, it felt good to know that he was there with her... there was a certain ease to their beautiful union... a tranquil vibe, like no other. They just worked... things were just so easy... until they weren't.

The strange thing is, although Enrique has put her through everything he has... Kristie still feels that they have a good chance of making this work... and for some reason, right now, in this moment, she feels more positive about it than ever. She can't explain it, but for some reason, she is feeling a strong sense of certainty that they will reconcile in the not-too-distant future, maybe she's being naïve? Maybe she's been listening to Lisa's romantic ideals a little too much? But hope has stirred in her heart, and she really does feel that Enrique will find a way to finally face his demons... it's only a matter of time.

After a few moments, for the first time since she's been back to her apartment, she finds herself shifting from the balcony facing the ocean, and following the terrace around to the view of the bay and beyond; she hasn't been able to bring herself to do this since she's been back here... she couldn't bring herself to do this, because she can see Enrique's building from here, and she's stopped herself from dwelling on that. But tonight, she feels she needs to be closer to him than she ever has been, since she left six weeks ago.

As her eyes find the top three floors of his building located on Brickell Avenue, she looks out across the bay, trying to find a way to make things work between them... trying to find a way back to her man... the love of her life... her beautiful Cuban.

* * *

Enrique

Following a late business dinner, Enrique makes his way up to the penthouse. He feels like shit, but managed to hold it together enough to look professional for the meeting; he's always been good at carrying himself like everything is great and he has everything under control, which during this tragic time, he's grateful for.

Thankful that it's too late for the elevator attendants to be working, as he stands alone in the elevator, he looks at his reflection in the mirrored wall... he barely recognizes himself. He's his usual ultra-stylish self, with his custom-made designer suit and hair styled to perfection, but to him, he looks just as shit as he feels.

He skipped his workout again this morning, and he's not proud of it either; his workouts keep him marginally sane, and right now, he needs to spend some serious time in the gym to try to level this shit out. This stop-start routine is bullshit, and he needs to get a grip. He's always so rigid and controlled with his diet and fitness regime, but lately, he's let it go, and he's nothing short of agitated with himself for it. As he studies the shadow of himself looking back at him in the elevator mirror, he tells himself that he will get up at 4am tomorrow and get his sorry ass in the gym!

As he steps into the penthouse, he puts on some Otis Redding, and "(Sittin' On) the Dock of the Bay" begins to play. He makes some cafécito as he listens to the music; he's feeling more alone than ever tonight, for some reason.

As "Pain in My Heart," also by Otis Redding, begins to play, he waits for the coffee to brew, with every lyric hitting him like a ton of bricks. Here he is, once again, making late-night espresso for one... will he ever get used to this? He highly doubts it.

He pours the coffee and makes his way to the balcony, stopping by the humidor to get himself a cigar. As his playlist shuffles to "These Arms of Mine," he sits out on the terrace, high up in the sky, and lights his cigar, then inhales the smooth smoke. As he exhales, he glances around the penthouse, seeing visions of him and Kristie together, laughing, fooling around, cooking dinner together, eating out on the balcony, making love in front of the fire, on the sofa, on the balcony, against the wall, against every wall, and on the very counter he was leaning on, while he was waiting for the coffee to brew; he misses his girl so damn much... he misses her more than ever... he needs her... he needs to hold her... to kiss her... to tell her how much he loves her... to hear her tell him that she loves him... for her to look at him the way she does, making him melt every time... will he ever get to experience any of this again? Will he ever hold her again... to feel her warmth as he embraces her... he hopes he will... he really hopes, more than anything in the world.

As he sips his Cuban espresso and puffs on his cigar, his eyes find Kristie's apartment across the bay, just like they have done many times before. Once again, he feels a sense of comfort as he gazes out at the view.

With "These Arms of Mine" now playing on repeat, he continues to smoke his cigar, reminiscing about times they once shared... magical, beautiful, happy times that he will hold in his heart forever.

All he can do is pray that he will have the privilege of being able to make more memories like these in the future with the love of his life... he knows the answer lies with him, and he has faith that he will find a way to reunite with his soul mate, his one and only true love, his life, his world, his universe... his everything, Kristie Carrington.

Printed in Great Britain
by Amazon

30119531R00137